I0613054

Rosa Nouchette Carey

Uncle Max by Rosa Nouchette Carey

Vol. II

Rosa Nouchette Carey

Uncle Max by Rosa Nouchette Carey
Vol. II

ISBN/EAN: 9783743373853

Manufactured in Europe, USA, Canada, Australia, Japa

Cover: Foto ©Andreas Hilbeck / pixelio.de

Manufactured and distributed by brebook publishing software (www.brebook.com)

Rosa Nouchette Carey

Uncle Max by Rosa Nouchette Carey

BY

ROSA NOUCHETTE CAREY

AUTHOR OF 'NELLIE'S MEMORIES' 'NOT LIKE OTHER GIRLS' 'WEE WIFIE'

IN THREE VOLUMES

VOL. II.

LONDON

RICHARD BENTLEY & SON, NEW BURLINGTON STREET

Publishers in Ordinary to Her Majesty the Queen

1887

CONTENTS

OF

THE SECOND VOLUME.

UNCLE MAX.

CHAPTER XVII.

'WHY NOT TRUST ME, MAX?'

AX looked very discomposed when he saw Miss Hamilton ; he shook hands with her gravely, and sat down without saying a word. I wondered if it were my fancy, or if Miss·Hamilton had really grown perceptibly paler since his entrance.

'What does this mean, Uncle Max?' I asked gaily, for this sort of oppressive silence did not suit me at all. 'I understood that you and Mr. Tudor were dining at the Glynns' to-night.'

'Lawrence has gone without me,' he replied. 'I had a headache, and so I sent an excuse. but as it got better I thought I would come up and see how you were getting on.'

' A headache, Uncle Max!' looking at him rather anxiously, for I had never heard him complain of any ailment before. I had been dissatisfied with his appearance ever since I had come to Heathfield; he had looked worn and thin for some time, but to-night he looked wretched.

' Oh, it is nothing,' he returned quickly. ' Miss Hamilton, I hardly expected to find you here with Ursula. I thought you were all going to the Maberleys'.'

' Etta and Giles have gone,' she replied quietly. 'I ought not to be here, as Lady Betty is alone at Gladwyn; but Miss Garston persuaded me to remain; but it is getting late. I must be going,' rising as she spoke.

' There is not the slightest need for you to hurry,' observed Max; ' it is not so very late, and I will walk up with you to Gladwyn.'

Indeed, I hope you will do nothing of the kind,' she said hurriedly. ' Miss Garston, will you please tell him that there is no need, no need at all; indeed, I would much rather not.'

Miss Hamilton had lost all her repose of

manner ; she looked as nervous and shy as any schoolgirl when Max announced his intention of escorting her ; and yet how could any gentleman have allowed her to go down those dark roads alone ?

Perhaps Max thought she was unreasonable, for there was a touch of satire in his voice as he answered her.

' I certainly owe it to my conscience to see you safe home. What would Hamilton say if I allowed you to go alone ?—Ursula,' turning to me with an odd look, ' it is a fine starlight night ; suppose you put on your hat—a run will do you good ; and relieve Miss Hamilton's mind.'

' Yes, do come,' observed Miss Hamilton, in a relieved voice ; but as she spoke, her lovely eyes seemed appealing to him, and begging him not to be angry with her ; but he frowned slightly, and turned aside, and took up a book. How was it those two contrived to misunderstand each other so often ?   Max looked even more hurt than he had done at Gladwyn.

I was not surprised to find that when I left the room Miss Hamilton followed me, but I was hardly prepared to hear her say in a troubled voice :

' Oh ! how unfortunate I am. I would not have had this happen for worlds. Etta will —oh ! what am I saying ?—I am afraid Mr. Cunliffe is offended with me because I did not wish him to go home with me—but,' a little proudly and resentfully, ' he is too old a friend to misunderstand me, so he need not have said that.'

' I think Uncle Max is not well to-night,' I replied, soothingly. ' I never heard him speak in that tone before ; he is always so careful not to hurt people's feelings.'

' Yes, I know,' stifling a sigh, ' it is more my fault than his ; he is looking wretchedly ill—and—and I think he is a little offended with me about other things ; it is impossible to explain, and so he misjudges me.'

' Why do you not try to make things a little clearer ? ' I asked. ' Could you not say a word to him as we walk home ? Uncle Max is so good that I cannot bear him to be vexed about anything, and I know he is disappointed that you will not work in the school.'

' Yes, I know ; but you do not understand,' she returned gently. ' I should like to speak to him, if I dared, but I think my courage will fail ; it is not so easy as you think.' And then as we went downstairs, she took my arm, and I could feel that her hand was very cold. ' I wish he had not asked you to come, it shows he is hurt with me ; but all the same, I should have asked you myself.'

Uncle Max took up his felt hat directly he saw us, and followed us silently into the entry ; he did not speak as we went down the little garden together ; and as we turned into the road leading to the Vicarage it was Miss Hamilton who spoke first. She was still holding my arm, perhaps that gave her courage, and she looked across at Max, who was walking on my other side.

' Mr. Cunliffe, I am so sorry you were hurt with me the other night, when Etta spoke about the schools. I am not giving up work for my own pleasure—I loved it far too much ; but there are reasons.'

I heard Max give a quick, impatient sigh in the darkness.

' So you always say, Miss Hamilton ; you remember we have talked of this before. I have thought it my duty more than once to remonstrate with you about giving up your work, but one seems to talk in the dark; somehow you have never given me any very definite reasons—headaches—well, as though I did not know you well enough to be sure you are the last person to think of ailments.'

'Yes, but one's friends are over-careful; but still, you are right, it is not only that. Mr. Cunliffe, I wish you would believe that I have good and sufficient reasons for what I do, even if I cannot explain them. It makes one unhappy to be misunderstood by one's clergyman, and,' hesitating a moment, 'and one's friends.'

'Friends are not left so completely in the dark,' was the pointed answer. 'It is no use, Miss Hamilton. I find it impossible to understand you. I have no right to be hurt. No, of course not. no right at all'—and here Max laughed unsteadily—'but still, as a clergyman, I thought it could not be wrong to remonstrate when my best worker deserted her post.'

There was no response to this, only Miss Hamilton's hand lay a little heavily on my arm as though she were tired. I thought it best to be silent. No word of mine was needed. I could tell from Max's voice and manner how bitterly he was hurt.

But when he next spoke it was on a different subject.

'I must beg your pardon, Miss Hamilton, for having wronged you in my thoughts about something else. I find your brother has forbidden you to attend evening service for the present. And no doubt he is right; but your cousin gave me to understand that you stayed away for a very different reason.'

'What did Etta tell you?' she asked quickly. But before he could answer a dark figure seemed to emerge rather suddenly from the roadside. Miss Hamilton dropped my arm at once. 'Is that you, Leah? Have my brother and Miss Darrell returned from Maplehurst?' And I detected an anxious note in her voice.

'Yes, ma'am,' returned Leah civilly; 'and Miss Darrell seemed anxious at your being out so late, because you would take cold, and Master begged you would wrap up and walk very fast.'

'Oh! I shall take no harm,' returned Miss Hamilton, impatiently. 'Good-night, Miss Garston, and thank you for a very happy evening. Good-night, Mr. Cunliffe, and thank you, too. There is no need to come any farther; Leah will take care of me.' And she waved her hand and moved away in the darkness.

'What a bugbear that woman is!' I observed, rather irritably, as we retraced our steps in the direction of the Man and Plough, the little inn that stood at the junction of the four roads. Everything looked dark and eerie in the faint starlight. Our footsteps seemed to strike sharply against the hard, white road; there was a suspicion of frost in the air. When Max spoke, which was not for some minutes, he merely remarked that we should have a cold Christmas, and then he asked me if I would dine with him at the Vicarage on Christmas Day. He and Mr. Tudor would be alone.

'Christmas will be here in less than a fortnight, Ursula,' he went on, rather absently, but I knew he was not thinking of what he was saying. And when we reached the White Cottage he followed me into the parlour, sat down before the fire, and stretched out his hands to the blaze, as though he were very cold.

I stood and watched him for a moment, and then I could bear it no longer.

'Oh, Max!' I exclaimed, 'I wish you

would tell me what makes you look so wretchedly ill to-night. Even Miss Hamilton noticed it. I am sure there is something the matter.'

'Nonsense, child. What should be the matter?' But Max turned his face away as he spoke. 'I told you that I had a headache; but that is nothing to make a fuss about. Mrs. Drabble shall make me a good strong cup of tea when I get home.'

Max's manner was just a trifle testy, but I was not going to be repelled after this fashion. On the contrary, I put my hand on his shoulder and obliged him to look at me.

'It is not only a headache. You are un-happy about something; as though I do not see that. Max, you know we have always been like brother and sister, and I want you to tell me what has grieved you?'

That touched him, as I knew it would, for he had dearly loved his sister.

'I wish your mother were here now,' he returned in a moved voice. 'I wish poor Emmie were here; there were not many women like her. One could have trusted her with anything.'

'I think I am to be trusted too, Max.'

'Yes, yes, you are like her, Ursula. You
have got just the same quiet way. Your voice
always reminds me of hers. She was a dear,
good sister to me, more like a mother than
a sister. I think if she had lived she would
have been a great comfort to me now, Ursula.'

'I know I am not so good as my mother,
but I should like to be a comfort to you in her
place.'

I suppose Max's ear detected the suppressed pain in my voice, for as he looked at
me his manner changed; the old affectionate
smile came to his lips, and he put his hands
lightly on me, as though to keep me near him.
'You have been a comfort to me, my dear.
You and I have always understood each other.
I think you are as good as gold, Ursula.'

'Then why not trust me, Max? Why not
tell me what makes you so unhappy?'

'Little she-bear,' he said, still smiling, ' you
must not begin to growl at me after this
fashion, because I am somewhat hipped and
want a change. There is no need to be anxious
about me. A man in my position must have
his own and other people's difficulties to bear.

No, no, my dear, you have a wise head, but you are too young to take my burdens on your shoulders. What should you know about an old bachelor's worries?'

'An old bachelor,' I returned indignantly, 'when you know you are young and handsome, Max. How can you talk such nonsense?'

I could see he was amused at this.

'You must not expect me to believe that; a man is no judge of his own looks; but I never thought much about such things myself. I detest the notion of a handsome parson. There, we will dismiss the subject of your humble servant. I want to ask you a favour, Ursula.' And then I knew that all my coaxing had been in vain, and that he did not mean to tell me what troubled him and made him look so pinched and worn.

But, in spite of this preface, he kept me waiting for a long time, while he sat silently looking into the fire and stroking his brown beard.

'Ursula,' he began at last, still gazing into the red cavern of coals, as though he saw visions there, 'I want you and Miss Hamilton to be great friends. I am sure that she has taken to you, and she likes few people, and it will be very good for her to be with you.'

Max's speech took me somewhat by surprise. I had not expected him to mention Miss Hamilton's name.

'She is not happy,' he went on, 'and she is more lonely than other girls of her age. Miss Elizabeth is a nice bright little thing, but, as Lawrence says, she wants ballast; she is a child compared to Gladys—Miss Hamilton, I mean,' and here Max stammered a little nervously.

'No, you are right, she is not happy,' I returned quietly; 'she gives me the impression that she has known some great trouble.'

'Every one has his troubles,' he replied evasively, 'most people indulge in the luxury of a private skeleton. Now, I have often thought that Miss Hamilton and her sister would have been far happier without Miss Darrell— she has rather a peculiar temper, and I have often fancied that she has misrepresented things. It is always difficult to understand women, even the best of them,' with a smothered sigh, ' but I confess Miss Darrell is rather a problem to me.'

'I am not surprised to hear you say that,' I returned quickly, 'you are just the sort of man, Max, to be hoodwinked by any designing person. I am less charitable than you, and women are sharper in these matters. I have already found out that Miss Darrell makes Miss Hamilton miserable.'

' Gently, gently, Ursula,' in quite a shocked voice ; ' there is no need to put things quite so strongly—you are rather hasty, my dear. Miss Darrell may be a little too managing, and perhaps jealous and exacting ; but I think she is very fond of her cousins.'

' Indeed,' rather dryly, for I did not agree with Max in the least; he was always ready to believe the best of every one.

' Hamilton, too, is really devoted to his sisters, but they do not understand him. I believe Miss Hamilton is very proud of her brother, but she does not confide in him. He has often told me, in quite a pained way, how reserved they are with him. I believe Miss Darrell is far more his confidante than his sisters.'

' No doubt,' I returned, quite convinced in my own mind that this was the case.

' So you must see yourself how much Miss

Hamilton needs a friend,' he went on hurriedly.
'I want you to be very good to her, Ursula;
perhaps you may think it a little strange if I
say that I think it will be as much your duty
to befriend Miss Hamilton as to minister to
Phebe Locke.'

'I wonder who is speaking strongly now,
Max.'

'But if it be the truth,' he pleaded a little
anxiously.

'You need not fear,' was my answer: 'if
Miss Hamilton requires my friendship, I am
very willing to bestow it. I will be as good to
her as I know how to be, Max—is it likely I
should refuse the first favour you have ever
asked me?' and as he thanked me rather
gravely, I felt that he was very much in earnest
about this. He went away after this, but I
think I had succeeded in cheering him, for he
looked more like himself as he bade me good-
night: but after he had gone I sat for a long
time, reflecting over our talk.

I felt perplexed and a little saddened by
what had passed. Max had not denied that
he was unhappy, but he had refused to confide
in me. Was his unhappiness connected in any

way with Miss Hamilton? This question baffled me: it was impossible for me to answer it.

I could not understand his manner to her. He was perfectly kind and gentle to her, as he was to all women, but he was also reserved and distant; in spite of their long acquaintance, for he had visited at Gladwyn for years, there was no familiarity between them. Miss Hamilton, on her part, seemed to avoid him, and yet I was sure she both respected and liked him. There was some strange barrier between them that hindered all free communication. Max was certainly not like himself when Miss Hamilton was present; and on her side, she seemed to freeze and become unapproachable the moment he appeared. But this was not the only thing that perplexed me, the whole atmosphere of Gladwyn was oppressive. I had a subtle feeling of discomfort whenever Miss Darrell was in the room; her voice seemed to have a curious magnetic effect on one, its tuneless vibrations seemed to irritate me; if she spoke loudly, her voice was rather shrill and unpleasant. She knew this, and carefully modulated it. I used to wonder over its smoothness and fluency.

And there was another thing that struck me. Mr. Hamilton seemed fond of his step-sisters, but he treated them with reserve; the frank jokes that pass between brothers and sisters, the pleasant raillery, the blunt speeches, the interchange of confidential looks, were missing in the family circle at Gladwyn. Mr. Hamilton behaved with old-fashioned courtesy to his sisters; he was watchful over their comfort, but he was certainly a little stiff and constrained in his manner to them,—he seemed to unbend more freely to his cousin than to them; he had scolded her, good-humouredly, once or twice, after quite a brotherly fashion; and she had taken his rebukes in a way that showed they understood each other. I grew tired at last of trying to adjust my ideas on the subject of the Hamilton family. I was rather provoked to find how they had begun to absorb my interest. 'Never mind, I have promised Uncle Max to be good to her,' was my last waking thought that night, 'and I am determined to keep my word.' And I fell asleep, and dreamt that I was trying to save Miss Hamilton from drowning, and that all the time Miss Darrell was standing on the shore laughing and pelting us with stones, and when a larger one than usual struck me, I awoke.

I wondered if it were accident or design that brought Miss Darrell across my path the next day. I had just left the Lockes' cottage, feeling somewhat tired and depressed—Phebe had been in one of her contrary moods, and had given me a good deal of trouble, but the evil spirit had been quieted at last, and I had taken my leave after reprimanding her severely for her rudeness. I was just closing the garden gate, when Miss Darrell came up to me in the dusk, holding out her hand with her tingling little laugh.

'How odd that we should have met just here ! I hardly knew you, Miss Garston, in that long cloak, you looked so like a Sister of Charity. I think you are very wise to adopt a uniform.'

'Thank you, but I have hardly adopted one,' I returned, folding the fur edges of my cloak closer to me, for it was a bitterly cold evening : 'are you going home, Miss Darrell ? because you have passed the turning that leads to Gladwyn.'

'Oh, I do not mind a longer round,' was

the careless answer. 'I am very hardy, and a walk never hurts me—if it were Gladys now, —by the bye, have you seen my cousin Giles to-day?'

'No!' I returned, wondering a little at her question.

'You are lucky to have escaped him,' with another laugh. 'Dear, dear, how angry Giles was last night, to be sure, when we came home and found Gladys out; he was far too angry to say much to her, he only asked her if she had taken leave of her senses, and that some people —I do not know whom he meant—ought to be ashamed of themselves.'

'Indeed!' somewhat sarcastically, for I confess this speech made me feel rather cross. I wondered if Mr. Hamilton could really have said it. I determined that I would ask him on the first opportunity.

'It was a very injudicious proceeding,' went on Miss Darrell, smoothly. 'Gladys was to blame, of course; but still, if you remember, I told you how delicate she was, and how we dreaded night air for her—young people are so careless of their health; but, of course, as Giles said, we thought she would be safe with you.

You see, Giles looks upon you in the character of nurse, Miss Garston, and forgets you are young too. " Depend upon it, they have forgotten the time," I said to him ; " when two girls are chattering their secrets to each other, they are not likely to remember anything so sublunary." You should have seen Giles's expression of lordly disgust when I said that.'

' I should rather have heard Mr. Hamilton's answer.'

' Don't be too sure of that,' returned Miss Darrell, in a mocking voice that somehow recalled my dream. ' I am afraid it would not please you—Giles is no flatterer. He said he thought you would have been far too sensible for that sort of nonsense, but that one never knew, and that it was not only young and pretty girls like Gladys who could be romantic, and for all your staid looks you were not Methuselah ; rather a dubious speech, Miss Garston.'

' True ! ' far too dubious to be entirely palatable to my feminine pride ; but I was careful not to hint this to Miss Darrell, and she went on in the same light jesting way.

' It is terribly hard to satisfy Giles, he is so

critical; he sets impossible standards for people, and then sneers if they do not reach it. He had conceived rather a high opinion of you, Miss Garston. He told me one day that he would be glad for you to be intimate with his sisters, as they would only learn good from you, and that he hoped that I would encourage your visits—I trust that he has not changed his opinion since then; but Giles is so odd when people disappoint him. I said last night that we would invite you for to-morrow, and then you and Gladys could finish your talk; but he was as cross as possible, and begged that I would invite no one for Thursday, as he was very busy, and Gladys must find another opportunity for her talk. There, how I am chattering on—and perhaps I ought not to have said all that; but I thought you would wonder at our want of neighbourliness—and of course we cannot expect you to understand Giles's odd temper; it is a great pity he has got this idea in his head.'

'What idea, Miss Darrell?'

'Dear, dear, how sharp you are; how you take me up. Of course it is only Giles's ill-temper, he cannot really think you wanting in ballast.'

' Oh, I understand now, please go on.'

' But I have no more to say,' rather bewildered by my abruptness; ' of course we
shall see you soon, when all this has blown
over. If you like, I will tell Giles I have seen
you.'

' Please tell Mr. Hamilton nothing, I will
speak to him myself. Good-night, Miss Darrell ;
I am rather cold and tired after my day's
work. I do not in the least expect that Miss
Hamilton has taken any harm,' and I made
my escape. I do not know what Miss Darrell
thought of me, but she walked on rather
thoughtfully ; as for me, I felt tingling all over
with irritation—if Mr. Hamilton had dared to
imply these things of me, I should hardly be
able to keep my promise to Uncle Max, for I
would certainly decline to visit at Gladwyn.

CHAPTER XVIII.

MISS HAMILTON'S LITTLE SCHOLAR.

MISS DARRELL'S innuendoes were not to be borne with any degree of patience. Mr. Hamilton's opinion might be nothing to me—how often I repeated that—but all the same, I owed it to my dignity to seek an explanation with him.

The opportunity came the very next day.

He called to speak to me about a new patient, a little cripple boy who had broken his arm; the father was a labourer, and there were ten children, and the mother took in washing. 'Poor Robin has not much chance of good nursing,' he went on; 'Mrs. Bell is not a bad mother, as mothers go, but she is overworked and overburdened; she has a good bit of difficulty in keeping her husband out of the alehouse.

Good heavens! what lives these women lead; it is to be hoped that it will be made up to them in another world—no washing-tubs and ale-houses there, no bruised bodies and souls, eh, Miss Garston?'

Mr. Hamilton was talking in his usual fashion; he had taken the arm-chair I had offered him, and seemed in no hurry to leave it, although his dinner hour was approaching. When he had given me full directions about Robin, and I had promised to go to him directly after my breakfast the next morning, I said to him in quite a careless manner that I hoped Miss Hamilton was well and had sustained no ill effects from her visit to me.

'Oh, no! she is better than usual. I think you roused her and did her good. Gladys mopes too much at home. All the same,' in a tolerant tone, 'you ought not to have kept her so late; as Etta very wisely remarked—it was no good for her to stay in on Sundays and remain out a couple of hours later another night; you see Gladys takes cold so easily.'

'I hear you were very much inclined to blame the village nurse, Mr. Hamilton.'

'Who—I?' looking at me in a little surprise.

'I do not remember that I said anything very dreadful. Etta was in a fuss as usual—you managing women like to make a fuss sometimes —she sent off Leah, and wanted me to lecture Gladys for her imprudence; but I was not inclined to be bothered, and said it was Gladys' affair if she chose to make herself ill, but all the same she ought to be ashamed of such skittishness at her age. I don't believe Gladys knew I was joking; that is the worst of her, she never sees a joke—Etta does though, for she burst out laughing when my lady walked off to bed in rather a dignified manner. I hope you are not easily offended too, Miss Garston?'

'Oh dear no,' I returned coolly, 'only I should be sorry if you had in any way changed your opinion of my steadiness. Miss Darrell hinted that you were vexed with me for keeping your sister, and thought that I was to blame.'

Mr. Hamilton looked so bewildered at this that I exonerated him from that moment.

'What nonsense has that girl been talking?' he said, rather irritated. 'I always tell her that tongue of hers will lead her into trouble; I know she talked plenty of rubbish that night.

When she said it was a pity that you and Gladys were always chattering secrets, I told her that though you were not a Methuselah, you were hardly the sort of person to indulge in that sort of sentimentality, that I could answer for your good sense in that; and that Etta need not be so hard on a pretty young girl like Gladys. That was not accusing you of want of steadiness.'

'No, thank you. I am so glad that I know what you really said.'

'Indeed, I was not aware that my good or bad opinion mattered to Miss Garston; you have certainly never given me the impression that you mind very much what I say or think.'

Was Mr. Hamilton cross? He looked quite moody all at once, his face wore that hard disagreeable look that I so disliked. He had been so pleasant in his manners ever since that evening at Gladwyn that I was rather sorry that this agreeable state of things should be disturbed. He was evidently not to blame for Miss Darrell's misrepresentations, so I hastened with much policy to throw oil on the troubled waters.

'I do not know why you should say that!

It ought not to be a matter of indifference what people think of us.'

'Ought it not—would you like to know my opinion of you after nearly a month of acquaintance? Let me warn you, I have entirely changed my opinion since our stormy interview in Cunliffe's study.'

I do not know what there was in Mr. Hamilton's look and manner that made me say hastily—

'Oh no, I would rather not know, and I hope you will not tell me. I am quite sure you do not misconstrue my motives now.'

'You may be quite sure of that,' rather grimly, as though my last speech displeased him. 'It is difficult not to think you older than you are, you are so terribly sensible and matter-of-fact; how can Gladys get on with you, I wonder? Do you put a moral extinguisher on all her romance?'

'I am not quite so matter-of-fact as you make out, Mr. Hamilton.'

He shot an odd sort of glance at me. 'When you sing one can believe that; there is nothing prosaic in a nest full of larks. Poor Phebe, I do believe you are doing her good—she looks

far more human already. By the bye, when
are you coming to sing to us again? I told
Etta that I was engaged on Thursday, and
she declared it was our only free day until
Christmas.'

'I shall be too busy to come till after then,'
I replied quietly, for I did not wish him to
think that I was ready to jump at any invitation
to Gladwyn. He seemed rather disconcerted
at my coldness.

'Why, it is more than ten days to Christmas! I hope you do not mean to be stiff and
unneighbourly, Miss Garston. I am afraid,'
with a decidedly quizzical look, 'that pride
is a serious defect of yours.'

'Perhaps so; but you see I do not wish to
be different from my neighbours,' I replied
quietly; but my speech was received by Mr.
Hamilton with a hearty laugh.

'Oh yes, you are right, we are a proud lot,'
he observed, as he rose to take leave. 'Well,
Miss Garston, after Christmas is over, we shall
hope to see you for an evening; but any afternoon you are free they will be glad to see you.
Etta makes excellent tea; what a craze five-
o'clock tea is with you women! I have pro-

tested against it in vain, the girls are in majority against me.' With this speech he took himself off. I was much relieved at this peaceable ending to our interview. Now he was gone I could scarcely believe that I had ventured on a joke with the formidable Mr. Hamilton, a joke which he had taken in excellent part. I began to feel less in awe of him, he certainly knew how to shake hands heartily, and I could recapitulate Lady Betty's criticism on myself and apply it to him, for when Mr. Hamilton smiled he looked quite a different man—years younger, and much better looking. Well, I was glad that he had such a good opinion of my common sense.

My hands were likely to be full of business until after Christmas. Mrs. Marshall was growing gradually weaker, and Mr. Hamilton was doubtful whether she would last to see the New Year in. Her husband would be home on Christmas Eve; his work at Lewes would be finished by then, and he hoped to find work nearer home. Poor Mary told me this with tears in her eyes; her one prayer was that she might be spared to see Andrew again. 'He has been a good husband to me, and has kept out

of the public-house for the sake of his wife and
the children, and I cannot die easy until I have
said good-bye to him,' finished the poor woman;
but when I repeated this to Mr. Hamilton he
shook his head—'A few hours may take her
off any day,' he said; 'it is only a wonder that
she has lasted so long. I believe she is keeping
herself alive by the sheer force of her longing
to see her husband. Women are strange creatures, Miss Garston.'

My new patient was likely to give me
plenty of occupation. I found the poor little
fellow, looking very forlorn and dull, lying in a
dark corner of a large chilly garret, which was
evidently shared by two or three brothers.

Mrs. Bell, who had left her washing-tub to
accompany me upstairs, stood drying her arms
on her apron, and talking in a high-pitched
querulous voice. 'No one can say I have not
been unfortunate this year,' she grumbled.
'There's Bell, he gets worse and worse. I
fetched him myself out of the Man and
Plough last Saturday night, where he was
drinking the money that was to buy the children bread. "Do you call yourself a man or a
brute?" I says, but in my opinions it's wronging

the poor bruteses to compare them with such as him. "Work," says he, "why don't you work yourself?" when I am at that wash-tub from morning till night.'

'And now poor Robin is adding to your trouble, Mrs. Bell,' I observed, with a pitying look at the child's white face and large wistful eyes.

'Ay, he has gone and done it now,' she returned, with a touch of motherly feeling; 'it was a slide those bad boys had made, and Robbie came down on it with his crutch under him. He is always in trouble, is Robbie, has had more illnesses than all the children put together; there is nothing Robin can't take— whooping-cough—why he nearly whooped himself to death; measles and scarlet fever— why he was as nearly gone as possible, the doctor said. He has always been puny and weakly from a baby. But there's Bell now makes more of a fuss over Rob than over the others; if it is anything that will keep him away from the Man and Plough, it is Rob asking him to take him out some- where.'

'Ay, father's promised to sit with me this

evening,' observed Robin, in a faint little treble.

'Then we must make the room comfortable for father,' I said quickly. 'Mrs. Bell, I must not hinder you any more; but if you could spare one of the girls to help me tidy up a little.'

'Ay, Sally can come,' she returned; 'the place does look like a piggery. You see Tom and Ned and Willie sleep here along of Robin, and boys know nought about keeping a place tidy; Sally redds it up towards evening. But there, Doctor said Robbie must have a fire, and I've clean forgotten it; I will send up Sally with some sticks and a lump or two of coal.'

Mrs. Bell was not a bad sort of woman certainly, but like many of her class she was not a good manager; and when a woman has ten children, and a husband rather too fond of the Man and Plough, and is obliged to stand at her washing-tub for hours every day, one cannot expect to find the house in perfect order.

We had soon a bright little fire burning which gave quite a cheery aspect to the large bare attic—the sloping roof and small window did not seem to matter so much. With Sally's help I moved Robin's little bed to a lighter part of the room, where the roof did not slope so much, and where the wintry sunlight could reach him. Robin seemed much pleased with this change of position, and when I had washed and made him comfortable he declared that he felt ' first-rate.'

I had so much to do for my patient that I was obliged to let Sally tidy up the room in her usual scrambling way; the child had been sadly neglected by that time, and he was getting faint. I had to prepare some arrow-root for his dinner, and then hurry off to the Marshalls' before I had my own. I was obliged to omit my visit to Phebe that day, and divide my time between Mrs. Marshall and Robin. When I had given Robin his tea, and had put a chair by the fire for father, I went off, feeling that I could leave him more comfortably. The eldest boy, Tom, a big, strapping lad of fourteen, who went to work, had promised to keep the other boys quiet, ' that the little chap might not be disturbed,' and as Robin again declared that he felt first-rate, if it weren't for his arm, I hoped that he might be able to sleep.

'Father stopped with me ever so long, until the boys came to bed,' were Robin's first words the next morning ; 'and Doctor came, and said we looked quite snug, and he is going to send father some books to read, and some papers, and father said he was more comfortable than downstairs, as I did not mind his pipe, and Tom has hung my linnet there,' pointing to the window, ' and if you open the cage, Miss, you will see him hop all over the bedclothes, and chirp in the beautifullest way.'

We had a great deal of cleaning to do that day. I shall never forget Lady Betty's face when she came upstairs and saw me down on my knees at work in my corner of the room ; for Sally was little, and the room was large, and I was obliged to go to her assistance.

' Good gracious, Miss Garston ! ' she said, in quite a shocked voice, ' you do not mean to tell me that you consider it your duty to scrub floors ! '

' Well, no,' I returned, laughing, for really her consternation was ludicrous. ' I should consider it a waste of strength, generally, but we never know what comes in a day's work. Sally is so little that I am obliged to help her.'

'Why can't Mrs. Bell do it?' asked Lady Betty, indignantly.

'Mrs. Bell has hardly time to cook the children's dinner. Please don't look so shocked. I don't often scrub floors, and I have nearly finished now. What have you brought in that basket, little Red Riding Hood?' for in her little crimson hood-like bonnet she did not look so unlike Red Riding Hood.

'Oh, Giles asked Gladys to send some things for poor little Robin, and she packed them herself. There is a jar of beef-tea, and some jelly, and some new-laid eggs, and sponge-cakes, and a roll or two; and Gladys hopes you will let her know what Robin wants, for he used to be her little scholar, and she is so interested in him.'

Of course I knew Lady Betty would chatter about me when she returned home, but I was rather vexed when Mr. Hamilton took me to task the next morning, and gave me quite a lecture on the subject; he made me promise at last that I would never do anything of the kind again. I hardly know what made me so submissive. I think it was his threat of keeping any more patients from me, and then he seemed so thoroughly put out.

'It is such folly wearing yourself out like this, Miss Garston,' he said angrily. 'I wonder why women never will learn common sense; if you work under me I will thank you to obey my directions, and I do not choose my nurse to waste her time and strength in scrubbing floors. Yes, Robin boy, I am very angry with nurse; but there is no occasion for you to cry about it—and—why, good heavens! if you are not crying too, Miss Garston. Of course, —there I told you so—you have just knocked yourself up.'

His tone so aggravated me that I plucked up a little spirit.

'I am not a bit knocked up'—and in rather a choky voice, 'I am not crying; I never cry before people; only I am a little tired. I was up all last night with Mrs. Marshall, and you talk so much.'

'Oh, very well,' rather huffily, but he was in a bad humour that day. 'I won't talk any more to you, but I should like to know one thing—when are you going home?'

'In another hour; my head aches rather, and I think I shall lie down.'

'Of course your head aches; but there, you have given me a promise, so I will not say any more. Try what a good nap will do. I am going round by the Lockes, and I shall tell Phebe not to expect you this afternoon. It won't hurt her to miss you sometimes; it will teach her to value her blessings more, and people cannot sing when they have a head-ache—' and he walked off without waiting for me to thank him for his thoughtfulness. What did he mean by saying that I was crying, the ridiculous man, just because there were tears in my eyes? I certainly could not fancy myself crying because Mr. Hamilton scolded me!

I had a refreshing nap, and kept my dinner waiting, but I must own I was a little touched when Mrs. Barton produced a bottle of champagne which she said Mr. Hamilton had brought in his pocket, and had desired that I was to have some directly I woke. 'And I was to tell you, with his compliments, that his sister Gladys would sit with Robin all the afternoon, and that Lady Betty was at the Marshalls', and he was going again himself, and Phebe Locke was better, and he hoped you would not stir out again to-day.'

How very kind and thoughtful of Mr. Hamilton—he has sent his sisters to look after my patients, that I might be able to enjoy my rest with a quiet conscience. I was sorry that he should think that I was so easily knocked up; but it was not over-fatigue nor yet his scolding that had brought the tears to my eyes. To-day was the second anniversary of Charlie's death, and through that long, wakeful night, as I sat beside poor Mary's bed, I was recalling the bitter hours when my darling went down deeper into the place of shadows—when he fought away his young life, while Lesbia and I wept and prayed beside him. No wonder a word unnerved me, but I could not tell Mr. Hamilton this.

When we met the next day he asked me, rather curtly, if the headache had gone; but when I thanked him, somewhat shyly, for the medicine he had sent, he got rather red, and interrupted me with unusual abruptness.

'You have nothing for which to thank me,' he said, in quite a repellent tone. 'I am glad you obeyed orders, and stopped at home; I was afraid you might be contumacious, as usual,' which was rather ungracious of him, after the promise he had extracted from me.

I questioned Robin about Miss Hamilton's visit; she had remained with the boy some hours, reading to him and amusing him, and in Robin's favourite language 'getting on first-rate; only, just as I was drinking my mugful of tea, Parson comes, and Miss Hamilton she says she will be late, and gets up in a hurry, and——'

'Wait a minute, Robin; do you mean Mr. Cunliffe or Mr. Tudor?'

'Oh, the Vicar, to be sure; and he seemed finely surprised to see Miss Hamilton there. "So you've come to see your old scholar," he says, smiling, and Miss Hamilton says, "Yes; but she must go now," and she drops her glove, and Parson looks for it, but it was too dark, and for all his groping it could not be found. "I must just go without it," says Miss Hamilton; "but I have got my muff, and it does not matter," and she says good-bye, and goes away. Parson found it, though,' went on Robin, garrulously. 'When Sally lighted the candle he spies it at once, and puts it in his pocket. "Miss Hamilton will be fine and glad when you tell her it is found," I says to Parson; but he just looks at me in an odd sort of way, and says, "Yes, Robin, certainly." "And you won't forget to give it to her, to-morrow, sir," but he did not seem to hear me. " Good-night, my man," he said. " So Miss Hamilton did not think you were too old to be kissed," and he kissed me just in the same place as she did. What did you say, miss?'

'I did not say anything, Robin.'

' Didn't you, miss? I thought I heard you say "poor man," or something like that. Is not Miss Hamilton beautiful? I think she is almost as beautiful as my picture of the Virgin Mary. I asked Parson if he did not think so, and he said yes. Do you think she will come again, soon?'

' We shall see, Robbie, dear.' But as I spoke something told me that we should not see Miss Hamilton there again!

CHAPTER XIX.

THE PICTURE IN GLADYS' ROOM.

THE days flew rapidly by, and I was almost too busy to heed them as they passed. Each morning I woke with fresh energy to my day's work; the hours were so full of interest and varied employment that my evening rest came all too soon. I grew so fond of my patients, especially of poor little Robin, that I never left them willingly; and the knowledge that I was necessary to them, that they looked to me for relief and comfort, seemed to fill my life with sweetness.

As I said to myself daily, no one need complain that one's existence is objectless, or altogether desolate, as long as there are sick bodies and sick souls to which one can minister. For 'Give, and it shall be given unto you,' is

the Divine command, and sympathy and help
bestowed on our suffering fellow-creatures shall
be repaid into our bosoms a hundredfold.   I
was right in my surmise—Miss Hamilton did
not again visit her little scholar; but Lady
Betty came almost daily, and was a great help
in amusing the child.   I was with him for an
hour in the morning, and again in the late
afternoon; but Mrs. Marshall took up the
greater part of my time ; she was growing
more feeble every day, and needed my constant care.   Unless it were absolutely necessary
I was unwilling to sacrifice my night's rest, or
to draw too largely on my stock of strength ;
but I had fallen into the habit, during the last
week or two, of going down to the cottage in
the evening about eight or nine, and settling
her comfortably for the night.   I found these
late visits were a great boon to her, and seemed
to break the length of the long winter night,
and so I did not regret my added trouble.
Poor Phebe had to be content with an hour
snatched from the busier portion of the day ;
but she was beginning to occupy herself now.
I kept her constantly supplied with books ; and
Miss Locke assured me that she read them with

avidity; her poor famished mind, deprived for so many years of its natural aliment, fastened almost greedily on the nourishment provided for it. From the moment I induced her to open a book her appetite for reading returned, and she occupied herself in this manner for hours.

She never spoke to her sister about what she had read, but when Kitty and she were alone she would keep the child entranced for an hour together by the stories she told her out of Miss Garston's books.

'Sometimes Kitty sings to her, and sometimes they have a rare talk,' Miss Locke would say. 'I am often too busy to do more than look in for five minutes or so, to see how they are getting on. Phebe grumbles far less; it is wonderful to hear her say, sometimes, that she did not know it was bedtime, when I go in to fetch the lamp. Reading—ay, she is always reading; but she sleeps a deal, too.'

I used to look round Phebe's room with satisfaction now; it had quite lost its stiff, angular look. A dark crimson foot-quilt lay on the bed, a stand of green growing ferns was on the table, and two or three books were always placed beside her.

Some gay china figures that I had hunted out of the glass cupboard in the parlour enlivened the mantelpiece, and a simple landscape, with sheep feeding in a sunny field, hung opposite the bed; some pretty cretonne curtains had replaced the dingy dark ones. Phebe herself had a soft fleecy grey shawl drawn over her thin shoulders. Mr. Hamilton again and again commented on her improved appearance, but I always listened rather silently; the evil spirit that had taken possession of Phebe had not finally left her; 'and why could not we cast it out?' used to come to my lips sometimes as I looked at her; but all the same I knew the Master-hand was needed for that.

Christmas Day fell this year on a Tuesday. On Sunday afternoon I had finished my rounds and was returning home to tea, when, as I was passing the Marshalls' cottage, Peggy ran after me bareheaded to say her father had just arrived, and would I come in for a moment, as mother seemed a little faint, and Grannie was frightened.

I hastened back with the child; for, of course, in poor Mary's state the least shock might prove fatal. I found Marshall stooping over the bed and supporting his wife with clumsy fondness, with the tears rolling down his weather-beaten face.

'I'm most 'feard she's gone, Missis,' he said hoarsely. 'Poor lass, I took her too sudden, and she had not the strength of the little 'un there.'

I bade him lay her down gently, and then applied the necessary remedies, and to my great relief my patient presently revived. It was touching to see the weak hand trying to feel for her husband; as it came into contact with the rough coat-sleeve, a smile came upon the deathlike face.

'It is Andrew himself,' she whispered ; 'I feared it was nought but a dream, mother; it is Andrew's own self, and he is looking well and hearty. Ay, lad,' with a loving look at him, 'I could not have died in peace till I had seen you again ; and now God's will be done, for He has been good to me and granted me my heart's desire.'

Poor Marshall looked weary and travel-stained, so I beckoned Peggy out of the room, and with her help there was soon a comfortable meal on the table; part of the meat-pie that was left from the children's dinner, a round or two of hot toast, and a cup of smoking coffee.

The poor man looked a little bewildered when he saw these preparations for his comfort, he wiped his eyes again with his rough coat-sleeve.

'I have been so long without wife or child that I can't make it out to see them all flocking round me again. There is Tim a man almost. Well, I have been tramping it since five this morning, and I am nearly ready to drop, so thank you kindly, Missis, and with your leave I will fall to.'

When I returned to Mary I found her looking wonderfully revived and cheerful.

'Isn't it grand to think that the Lord has let me have my own way about seeing Andrew?' she said, with a smile; 'he will be here now, poor lad, to see the last of me and look after the children. Now, you must not let me keep you, Miss Garston, for Andrew is that handy he can nurse as well as mother there before she lost her eyesight. I have been a deal of trouble to you, and now you must go home and rest.'

I was glad to be set at liberty, for I hoped that I might be in time to attend evening service; but just as I had finished tea, and was trying to think that I was not so very tired, and that it would not be wiser to stay at home, the outer door unlatched, and the next moment there was a quick tap at the parlour door, and Lady Betty bustled in looking very rosy from the cold.

'Oh! I can't stop a moment,' she said breathlessly; 'I have given Etta the slip, and in five minutes she will be looking for me; but I took it in my head to ask you to go and see Gladys. She is in her room with a cold, and looks dreadfully dull, and I know it will do her so much good if you will go and talk to her. Giles is out and every one else, so no one will disturb you; so do go, there's a good soul.' And actually before I could answer the impetuous little creature had shut the door in my face, and I could hear her running down the garden path.

I had not seen Miss Hamilton since the evening Uncle Max discovered us together, and I could not resist the temptation of finding her alone. Lady Betty had said she was in her room, and looked dreadfully dull. I had promised Max to be good to her, so, of course, it was my duty to go and cheer her up. I made this so plain to my conscience that in five minutes more I was on the road to Gladwyn, and before the church bells had stopped ringing I had entered the dark shubberies, and was looking at the closed windows wondering which of them belonged to Miss Hamilton's room.

I was agreeably surprised when a pretty-looking maid admitted me. I had taken a strange dislike to Leah, and the man who had waited upon us at dinner that evening had a dark unprepossessing face ; but this girl looked bright and cheerful, and took my message to Miss Hamilton at once without a moment's hesitation. She returned almost immediately. Miss Hamilton was in her room, but she would be very glad to see me, and the girl looked glad too as she led the way to the turret-room. Miss Hamilton was standing on the threshold, and met me with outstretched hands ; she looked ill and worn, and had a soft white shawl drawn closely round her as though she were chilly, but her eyes brightened at the sight of me.

'This is good of you, Miss Garston; I never expected such a pleasure. That will do, Chatty; you can close the door,' and still holding my hand she drew me into the room. It was a pretty room, but furnished far more simply than Miss Darrell's. The deep bay window formed a recess large enough to hold the dressing-table and a chair or two, and was half hidden by the blue cretonne curtains; besides this there were two more windows. Miss Hamilton had been sitting in a low cushioned chair by the fire; a small table with a lamp and some books were beside her; a Persian kitten lay on the white rug. On a stand beside a chair was a large beautifully painted photograph in a carved frame, the folding-doors were open, and a vase of flowers stood before it.

'What has put this benevolent idea into your head?' she asked, as she drew forward a comfortable wicker chair with a soft padded seat. 'I thought I had a long, dull evening before me, with no resource but my own thoughts, for I was tired of reading. I could scarcely believe Chatty when she said that you were in the drawing-room.'

I told Miss Hamilton of Lady Betty's visit, and she laughed quite merrily.

'Good little Betty. She is always trying to give me pleasure. She wanted to stay with me herself, only Etta said it was no use for two people to stop away from church. They have all gone, even Thornton and Leah. I believe only Parker and Chatty are in the house.'

'Is Chatty the housemaid?'

'No, the under-housemaid; but Catherine's father is ill, so she has gone to nurse him——'

'And Leah—who is Leah? I mean what is her capacity in the household?' as Miss Hamilton looked rather surprised at my question.

'She used to be Aunt Margaret's attendant, and now she is Etta's maid—at least, we call her so—but she makes herself useful in many ways. She is rather a superior person, and well educated, but I like Chatty to wait on me best; she is such a simple, honest little soul. I know people say servants have not much feeling, but I am sure Chatty would do anything for me and Lady Betty.'

'And you think Leah would not?' I asked rather stupidly.

E

'I did not say so, did I?' she answered quickly. 'We always look upon Leah as Etta's servant. She was devoted to her old mistress, and of course that makes Etta care for her so much. To me she is not a pleasant person. Etta has spoiled her, and she gives herself airs, and takes too much upon herself. Do you know'—with an amused smile—'Lady Betty and I think that Etta is rather afraid of her? She never ventures to find fault with her, and once or twice Lady Betty has heard Leah scolding Etta when something has put her out. I should not care to be scolded by my maid, should you, Miss Garston?'

'No,' I returned, rather absently, for, unperceived by Miss Hamilton, my attention was arrested by the photograph. It was the portrait of a young man, and something in the face seemed familiar to me.

The next moment I was caught. A distressed look crossed Miss Hamilton's face, and she made a sudden movement, as though she would close the photograph; but on second thoughts she handed it to me.

'Should you like to see it more closely? It is a photograph of my twin-brother, Eric.

They think—yes ! they are afraid that he is dead.'

Her lips had turned quite white as she spoke, and in my surprise, for I never knew there had been another brother, I did not answer, only bent over the picture.

It was the face of a young man about nineteen or twenty. A beautiful face that strangely resembled his sister's; the large blue-grey eyes were like hers, but the fair budding moustache scarcely hid the weak irresolute mouth. Here the resemblance stopped, for Miss Hamilton's firm lips and finely-curved chin showed no lack of power; but in her brother's face—attractive as it was—there were clearly signs of vacillation.

' Well, what do you think of it ? ' she asked, with a quick catch of her breath.

' It is a beautiful face,' I returned, rather hesitating. ' Very striking, too. One could not easily forget it ; and it is strangely like you ; but——' ·

' Yes, I know '—taking it out of my hand and closing the carved panels—' but you think it weak. Oh, yes, we cannot all be strong alike. Our Creator has ordained that, and it is for us to

E 2

LIBRARY
UNIVERSITY OF ILLINOIS

be merciful. Poor Eric! He would be three and twenty now. He was just twenty when that was taken.'

'And he is dead?'

'They say so. They think he is drowned, but we have no real proof—and we cannot be sure of it. He is alive in my dreams. That is the best of not really knowing,' she went on in a sad voice; 'one can go on praying for him, for, perhaps, after all, he may one day come back; not from the dead—oh no, I do not believe that for a moment; but if he be alive—' her eyes dilating and her manner full of excitement.

I pressed her to tell me about him, adding softly that I could feel for her more than any one else, as I had lost my own twin-brother. But she looked kindly at me and shook her head.

'Not to-night. I do not feel well enough, and it always makes me so ill and excited to speak about it, and we should not have time. Perhaps some day, when I get more used to you. Oh yes, some day, perhaps.'

'Indeed, I do not wish to intrude upon your trouble, Miss Hamilton,' I returned, colouring at this repulse. But she took my hand and pressed it gently.

'You must not be hurt with me. I have never spoken to any one about Eric. Mr. Cunliffe knows. But he—he—is different, and he was very kind to me. I must always be grateful.' The tears came into her eyes, and she hurried on :—

'I should like you to know, only I am such a coward. I am so sure of your sympathy, you seem already such a friend. Why do you call me Miss Hamilton? I am younger than you. I should like to hear you say Gladys. Miss Hamilton seems so stiff from you, and for years I have thought of you as Ursula.'

'You mean that Uncle Max has often talked of me?'

'Oh yes,' with an involuntary sigh, ' of you and your brother. He was always so fond of you both. He used to say very often that he wished that I knew you ; that you were so good, so unlike other people ; that you bore your trouble so beautifully.'

'I bore my trouble well! Oh, Miss Hamilton, it is impossible that he could have said that, when he knew how rebellious I was.' But here I could say no more.

'Don't cry, Ursula,' she said very sweetly ;

'you are not rebellious now. Oh! I used to be so sorry for you; you little thought that at that dreadful time, when you were so lonely and desolate, that a girl whom you had never seen, and perhaps of whom you had never heard, was praying for you with all her heart—that is what I mean by saying that I have known you for a long time.'

By mutual impulse we bent forward and kissed each other, a quiet lingering kiss that spoke of full understanding and sympathy. I had promised Uncle Max to be good to this girl, to do all I could to help her, but I did not know as I gave that promise how my heart would cleave to her, and that in time I should grow to love her with that rare friendship that is described in Holy Writ as 'passing the love of women.' We were silent for a little while, and then by some sudden impulse I began to speak of Max; I told her that I felt a little anxious about him, that he did not seem quite well or quite happy.

'I have thought so myself,' she returned, very quietly.

'Max is so good, that I cannot bear to see him unhappy—he is so unselfish, so full of thought for other people, so earnest in his work, so conscientious and self-denying.'

'True,' she replied, taking up a little toy screen that lay in her lap and shielding her face from the flame; 'he is all that. If any one deserves to be happy it is your uncle.'

I was glad to hear her say this, but her voice was a little constrained.

'He seems very far from happy just now,' was my answer; 'he looks worn and thin, as though he were overworking himself. I asked him the other night what ailed him. Are you cold, Miss Hamilton; I thought you shivered just now?'•

'No, no,' she returned, a little impatiently, ' you were speaking of your uncle.'

'Yes. I could not get him to tell me what was the matter; he began to joke—you know his way—men are so tiresome sometimes.'

'It is not always easy to understand them,' she said, turning away her face; 'perhaps they do not wish to be understood; it must be a great comfort to Mr. Cunliffe to have you so near him. I have thought lately that he has seemed a little lonely.'

'But he comes here very often,' I said,

rather quickly; 'he need not be dull with so many friends.'

To my surprise Miss Hamilton's fair face flushed almost painfully.

'He does not come so often as he used; perhaps he finds us a little too quiet. I am sorry for Giles's sake—oh, yes, I do not mean that,' as I looked at her rather reproachfully. 'Of course we all like Mr. Cunliffe.'

I was about to reply to this, when Miss Hamilton suddenly grew a little restless, and the next moment the door-bell sounded.

I rose at once. 'They have come back from church. I will bid you good-bye now,' and as I expected, she made no effort to keep me.

'You will come again,' she said, kissing me affectionately. 'I have so enjoyed our little talk; you have done me good, indeed you have, Ursula,' watching me from the threshold. I knew I could not escape my fate, so I walked downstairs as coolly as I could, and encountered them all in the hall. Miss Darrell gave a little shriek when she saw me.

'Dear me, Miss Garston, how you startled me! Who would have thought of finding you

here on Sunday evening, when all good people
are at church!' but here Mr. Hamilton put her
aside with little ceremony; he really seemed
as though he were glad to see me.

'You came to sit with Gladys—it was very
kind and thoughtful of you. Poor girl, she
seemed rather dull, but now you have cheered
her up.'

'Perhaps Miss Garston will extend her
cheering influence, Giles,' observed Miss
Darrell in her most staccato manner, 'and
remain to supper. Leah will see her home.'

'I am going to perform that office myself,
Etta. Will you stay?' looking at me in a
friendly manner.

'Not to-night,' I returned hurriedly; 'and,
indeed, I can very well walk alone;' but Mr.
Hamilton settled that question by putting on
his great-coat.

'Oh, of course Giles will walk with you;
how could he do less?' replied Miss Darrell, with
a scarcely perceptible sneer. 'You have timed
your visit so well that he will be just back to
supper. So you have been sitting with dear
Gladys—I wonder how you knew she had a
cold—private information, I suppose. I should

hardly have thought Gladys was well enough to see visitors, she was so feverish when I left her; but that stupid Chatty makes such mistakes.'

'Miss Hamilton was not at all feverish, I assure you. My visit has done her no harm,' and I turned to Lady Betty, who stood on tiptoe to kiss me, and breathed a 'thank you' into my ear; but Miss Darrell could not forbear from a parting fling as she bade me goodnight.

'We shall wait supper for you, Giles,' she said rather pointedly; but Mr. Hamilton took no notice; he only bade me be careful, as it was rather slippery by the gate, and then he began telling me about the sermon, and strangely enough he endorsed my opinion of Max.

'I tell him he must have a change after Christmas; he looks knocked up, and a trifle thin. It will not hurt Tudor to work a little harder; you may tell Cunliffe I say so. Halloa! I think you had better take my arm, Miss Garston, it is confoundedly dark and slippery'; but I declined this, as I was tolerably sure-footed.

Mr. Hamilton seemed in excellent spirits, and talked well and with great animation, as though he were bent on amusing me ; he was a clever man, and had a store of useful information which he did not always care to produce. I never heard him talk better than on this occasion, there were flashes of wit and brilliancy that surprised me, I was almost sorry when I reached the cottage.

'Good-night, Miss Garston, and thank you again for your deed of charity,' he said quite heartily, and as though he meant it. Really I never liked Mr. Hamilton so much before—but then he had never shown himself so genial. I saw Lady Betty the next morning and asked her after Miss Hamilton, but I almost regretted my question when the naughty little thing treated me to one of her usual confidences— there was no inducing her to hold her tongue when she was in the humour for chatting.

'Oh, it was such fun !' she said, her eyes dancing with mischief. 'Etta was so cross when you were gone ; she declared it was a conspiracy between us three, and that you only wanted Giles to walk home with you. No, I did not mean to repeat that, so please don't look so

angry. Etta did not really think so, but she
will say these things about people. I tell Gladys
Etta wants Giles herself. She scolded Chatty
for being so stupid, and said if Leah had been at
home she would have shown more sense; and
then she went up to Gladys' room in a nice
temper, but Gladys would not listen, said she
was tired, and ordered Etta out of the room.
When Gladys is like that Etta can do nothing
with her, so she sulked until Giles came home,
and then began teasing him about his gallantry,
and wondering how he enjoyed his walk, and
you know her way.'

'Lady Betty, I am busy; besides which I
do not wish to hear any more of your cousin's
improving conversation.'

'Oh, there is nothing more to tell,' she returned triumphantly. 'Giles silenced her so
completely that she did not dare to open her
lips again. Oh! she is properly frightened of
Giles when he is in one of his moods. He told
her that he disliked these sort of observations,
that in his opinion they were both undignified and
vulgar, especially when they related to a person
whom he so much respected as Miss Garston.
"And allow me to remark," he continued,

looking at poor little me rather fiercely, as though I were in fault too, "that I shall consider it an honour if Miss Garston bestows her friendship on any member of my household. I am very glad she seems to like Gladys, and I only hope she will do the poor girl good and come every day if she likes, and that is all I mean to say on the subject." But I think he said quite enough—don't you, Miss Garston?' finished naughty Lady Betty, looking up at me with such innocent eyes that I could not have scolded her any more than I could have scolded a kitten.

But if only Lady Betty could learn to hold her tongue——!

CHAPTER XX.

ERIC.

THAT afternoon I had rather an adventure. I was just walking up the hill on my way to the post office, when a handsome carriage came round the corner by the church rather sharply, and the same moment a little dog crossing the road in the dusk seemed to be under the horses' feet.

That was my first impression, my next was that the coachman was trying to pull up his horses. There was a sudden howl, the horses kicked and plunged, some one in the carriage shrieked, and then the little dog was in my arms, and even in the dim light I could feel one poor little leg was broken.

The horses were quieted with difficulty, and the footman got down and went to the carriage window.

'It is poor little Flossie, ma'am,' he said, touching his hat, 'she must have got out into the road and recognised the carriage, for she was under the horses' feet. This lady got her out somehow.' And indeed I had no idea how I had managed it. One of the horses had reared, and his front hoof almost touched me as I snatched up Flossie. I suppose it was a risky thing to do, for I never liked the remembrance afterwards, and I do not believe I could have done it again.

'Oh dear, oh dear,' observed a pleasant voice, 'do let me thank the lady. Stand aside, Williams,' and a pretty old lady with white hair looked out at me.

'I am afraid the poor dog's leg is broken,' I observed, as the little animal lay in my arms uttering short barks of pain; 'happily your man pulled up in time, or it must have been killed.'

'Oh dear, oh dear, what will the Colonel say to such carelessness?' exclaimed the old lady. 'He's so fond of Flossie, and makes such a fuss with her. And Mr. Hamilton has gone to Brighton, or I would have sent Flossie in for him to attend to her.'

'Will you let me see what I can do, Mrs.

Maberley,' I said, for I had recognised the pretty old lady at once. 'I am the village nurse, Miss Garston, and I think I can bind up poor Flossie's leg.'

'Miss Garston!' in quite a different voice, it seemed to have grown rather formal. 'Oh, I am so much obliged to you, but I am ashamed to give you the trouble; only for poor Flossie's sake,' hesitating, 'will you come into the carriage, and let me drive you to Maplehurst?' and to this I readily consented. I could never bear to see an animal in pain, and the little creature, a beautiful brown-and-white spaniel, was already licking my hand confidingly.

I could see Mrs. Maberley was embarrassed by my presence, for she talked in rather a nervous manner about it being Christmas Eve, and how busy the young ladies were decorating the church.

'I wanted to speak to Miss Darrell for a moment,' she went on, 'and I found her and Lady Betty putting up wreaths in the chancel, and that good-looking Mr. Tudor was helping them. I was so sorry poor dear Gladys was not there, but Miss Darrell says her cold is so much better that she is downstairs again. I am afraid she is very delicate and takes after her poor mother.'

'I saw Miss Hamilton yesterday, and I certainly thought she looked very ill.'

'So Miss Darrell told me. What a good, unselfish little creature she is, Miss Garston. I do not know what Mr. Hamilton and his sisters would do without her. Ah, here we are at Maplehurst, and Tracy is looking out for us. Tracy, is the Colonel at home? No, I am thankful to hear it. Poor little Flossie has met with an accident, and this lady has saved her life, but she tells me her leg is broken. Now, Miss Garston, will you believe it, that I am such a coward that I could not be of the least assistance? Tracy, take Miss Garston into the morning room, and do your best to help her;' and Mrs. Maberley trotted away as fast as she could, while Tracy ushered me into a bright snug-looking room, and asked me very civilly what she could do for me.

Tracy was a handy, sensible woman, and in a few minutes I had managed, with her help, to strap up poor Flossie's leg in the most successful manner.

'I am sure, ma'am, Mr. Hamilton couldn't

have done better himself,' observed Tracy, looking at me with respectful admiration, while I petted Flossie, who was now lying comfortably in her basket, trying to lick her bandages. 'I must go and tell my mistress that it is done, for she will be fretting herself ill over poor Flossie.'

I expect Tracy sounded my praises, for when Mrs. Maberley entered the room in her pretty cap with grey ribbons, there was not a trace of formality in her manner as she thanked me with tears in her eyes for my kindness to Flossie.

'To think of a young creature being so clever,' she said, folding her soft dimpled hands together. 'My dear, the Colonel will be so grateful to you; he dotes on Flossie. You must stay and have tea with me, and then he can thank you himself. No, I shall take no refusal. Tracy, tell Marvel to bring up the tea-tray at once. My dear,' turning to me, when Tracy had left the room, 'I am almost ashamed to look you in the face when I remember how long you have been in Heathfield, and that I have never called on you; but Etta told me that you did not care to have visitors.'

'Yes, I know, Mrs. Maberley, but that is quite a mistake,' I returned, somewhat eagerly, for I had fallen in love with the pretty old lady, and her tall, aristocratic colonel with his white moustache and grand military carriage, and had watched them with much interest from my place in church. She was such a dainty old lady, like a piece of Dresden china, with her pink cheeks and white curls, and old-fashioned shoe-buckles; and she had such beautiful little hands, plump and soft as a baby's, which she seemed to regard with innocent pride, for she was always settling the lace ruffles round her wrists, and pinching them up with careful fingers.

'Dear, dear! I thought Etta told me—' she began rather nervously.

'Miss Darrell makes mistakes, like other people,' I answered, smiling. 'I shall be very pleased to know my neighbours; but it is quite true that I am not often at home, and just now I am very busy, but all the same I do not mean to shut myself out from society. One owes a duty to one's neighbours.'

'My dear Miss Garston, I am quite pleased to hear you talk so sensibly. I was afraid from what Etta said that you were a little eccentric and strong-minded, and I have such a dislike to that in young people; young ladies are so terribly independent at the present day, in my opinion, and I know the Colonel thinks the same. They are sadly deficient in good manners and reverence; that is why I am so fond of the Hamilton girls, they are perfect young gentlewomen; they never talk slang or slipshod English, and they know how to respect grey hairs. The Colonel is devoted to Gladys; I tell him he is as fond of her as though she were his own daughter.'

'I think every one must be fond of Miss Hamilton.'

'Yes, poor darling, and she is much to be pitied,' returned Mrs. Maberley, with a sigh. 'Oh, here comes Marvel with the tea. Now, Miss Garston, my dear, take off that bonnet and jacket; I like people to look as though they were at home. Marvel, draw up that chair to the fire, and give Miss Garston a table to herself, and put the muffins where she can reach them; there, now I think we look comfortable—young people always look nicer without their bonnets; it was a pity to hide your pretty

smooth hair. Now tell me a little about yourself—I am sure Etta is wrong, you do not look
in the least strong-minded. Tracy said it was
wonderful how such slender little fingers could
ever do hospital work. She has fallen in love
with you, my dear, and Tracy has plenty of
penetration. I never can understand why she
does not take to Etta—and Etta is so good to
her ; but there, we all have our prejudices.'

As soon as Mrs. Maberley's ripple of talk
had died away I told her a little about my
work, and how much I liked my life at Heathfield, and then I spoke of my great interest in
Gladys Hamilton.

It was really very pleasant sitting in this
warm, softly-lighted room, and talking to this
charming, kind-hearted old lady. Christmas
Eve was not so dull after all as I had expected ; it
was nice to feel that I was making a new friend ;
that the little service I had rendered Mrs.
Maberley had broken down the barrier between
us and overcome her prejudice. I knew that
Miss Darrell had set her against me, and that
for some reason of her own she wished to
prevent her calling upon me.

Did Miss Darrell dislike my coming to

Heathfield? Was she afraid of finding me in her way? Was she at all desirous of making my stay irksome to me? These were some of the questions I was continually asking myself.

I noticed that Mrs. Maberley sighed and shook her head when I spoke of Miss Hamilton. As I warmed to my subject, and praised her beauty, and gentleness, and intelligence, she sighed still more.

'Yes, she is a dear girl, a dear good girl; but she has never been the same since Eric went—does she talk to you about Eric, Miss Garston? Etta says she talks of nothing else to her.'

I opened my eyes rather widely at this statement, for I could not forget what Miss Hamilton had said to me that night : ' I have never spoken to any one about Eric.' Was it likely that she would choose Miss Darrell for a confidante? But I kept my incredulity to myself, and simply related to Mrs. Maberley the circumstance that I had seen the photograph by accident the previous evening, and only knew then that Miss Hamilton had had a twin-brother.

'How very singular!' she observed, putting down her teacup in a hurry. 'I should have thought every one in the place would have spoken about the young man; he was such a favourite, and it was no use Mr. Hamilton trying to keep it a secret. Why the post-master's wife told me before Eric had been gone twenty-four hours, and then I went to Mr. Cunliffe. Why, child, do you mean your uncle has never told you about it?'

'Oh no, Uncle Max never repeats anything; he would be the last person from whom I should hear it.'

'And yet he was up at Gladwyn every day, ay, twice a day; and people said—— But what an old gossip I am! Well, about poor Eric, there can be no harm in your knowing what all the world knows, even Marvel and Tracy; it is a very sore subject with poor Mr. Hamilton, and no one dares to mention Eric's name to him; but, as Etta says, Gladys can never hold her tongue about him when they two are alone together.' I certainly held mine at that moment. I began to wonder what Miss Darrell would say next.

'So you have seen his picture, Miss Garston, my dear; well, now, is it not a beautiful face?—not sufficiently manly, as the Colonel says; but then, poor fellow, he had not a strong character. Still it was a lovely sight to see them together—our gardens join, you know; and often and often, as I have sat under our beech, I have seen Gladys and Eric walking up and down the little avenue, with his arm round her, and their two heads shining like gold, and she would be talking to him and smiling in his face, until it made me quite young to see them.'

'Wait a moment, Mrs. Maberley, please. I am deeply interested; but would Gladys— would Miss Hamilton like me to know all this?'

'To be sure, she would—though, perhaps, she would not care for the pain of telling it herself; but it would be better for you to hear it from me than from Mrs. Barton, or Mrs. Drabble, or any other gossiping person that takes it into her head to tell you, for you could not be much longer at Heathfield without hearing of it, when, as I say, every Jack and Tom in the village knows it—though how it all got about is more than I can say. I tell the

Colonel, Leah must have had a hand in it; I know it was she who told Tracy.'

I saw by this time that Mrs. Maberley had quite made up her mind to tell me the story herself; she was garrulous like many other old ladies, and perhaps she enjoyed a little gossip about her neighbours, so I only essayed one other feeble protest.

'I hope Mr. Hamilton will not mind'; but she answered me quite briskly—

'Well, poor fellow, he knows by this time people will talk; I daresay he thinks Mr. Cunliffe has told you. Now, I do not want to blame Mr. Hamilton; he is a great favourite of mine ever since he cured the Colonel's gout, and I would not be hard on him for worlds; but I have always been afraid that he did not rightly understand Eric; the brothers were so different. Mr. Hamilton is very hard-working and rather matter-of-fact, and Eric was quite different, more like a girl, dreamy and enthusiastic, and terribly idle, and then he fancied himself an artist. Mr. Hamilton could not bear that.'

'Why not? An artist's is a very good profession.'

'Yes, but he did not believe in his talent; and then Eric was intended for the law— his brother had sent him to Oxford; but he would not work, and he was extravagant, and got into debt—and, oh yes, there was no end of trouble. I do not know how it was,' went on Mrs. Maberley, 'but Eric always seemed in the wrong. Etta used to take his part, which was very good of her, as Eric could not bear her and treated her most rudely. Mr. Hamilton used to complain that Gladys encouraged him in his idleness; he sometimes came in here of an evening looking quite miserable, poor fellow, and say that his sisters and Eric were leagued against him; that but for Etta he would be at his wits' end what to do. Eric would not obey him, he simply defied his authority; he was growing more idle every day, and when he remonstrated with him, Gladys took his part. Oh dear, I am afraid they were all very wretched.'

'You think Mr. Hamilton did not understand his young brother.'

'Well, perhaps not. You see Mr. Hamilton had not the same temptations; he was always steady and hard-working from a boy, and never

cared much about his own comfort. As for
getting into debt, why, he would have considered
it wicked to do so. I know the Colonel thought
once or twice that he was a little hard on Eric.
I remember his saying once " that boys will be
boys, and that all are not good alike, and that
he must not use the curb too much." It was a
pity, certainly, that Mr. Hamilton was so angry
about his painting. I daresay it was only a
temporary craze. I am afraid, though, Eric
must have behaved very badly. I know he
struck his elder brother once. Anyhow, things
went on from bad to worse; and one day a
dreadful thing happened. A cheque of some
value, I have forgotten the particulars, was
stolen from Mr. Hamilton's desk, and the next
day Eric disappeared.'

' Was he accused of taking it ? '

' To be sure. Leah saw him with her own
eyes. You must ask Mr. Cunliffe about all
that, my memory is apt to be treacherous
about details. I know Leah saw him with his
hand in his brother's desk, and though Eric
vowed it was only to put a letter there—a very
impertinent letter that he had written to his
brother—still the cheque was gone, and, as they

heard afterwards, cashed by a very fair young man at some London bank; and the next morning, after some terrible quarrel, during which Gladys fainted, poor girl, Eric disappeared, and the very next thing they heard of him, about three weeks afterwards, was that his watch and some pocket-book belonging to him had been picked up on the Brighton beach close to Hove.'

'Do you mean that this is all they have ever heard of him?'

'Yes. I believe Mr. Hamilton employed every means of ascertaining his fate. For some months he refused to believe that he was dead. I am not sure if Gladys believes it now. But Etta did from the first. "He was weak and reckless enough for anything," she has often said to me. Of course, it is very terrible, and one cannot bear to think of it, but when a young man has lost his character he has not much pleasure in his life.'

'I do not think Miss Hamilton really believes that he is dead.'

'Perhaps not, poor darling. But Mr. Hamilton has no doubt on the subject, my dear Miss Garston. He is much to be pitied—he has

never been the same man since Eric went. I
am afraid that he repents of his harshness to
the poor boy. He told the Colonel once that
he wished he had tried milder treatment.'

'One can understand Mr. Hamilton's feelings
so well. You are right, Mrs. Maberley, he is
much to be pitied.'

'Yes, and to make matters worse, Gladys
was very ill, and refused to see or speak to him
in her illness. I believe the breach is healed between them now, but she is not all that a sister
ought to be to him.'

'Perhaps Miss Darrell usurps her place,' I
replied, a little incautiously, but I saw my mistake at once. Mrs. Maberley was evidently a
devout believer in Miss Darrell's merits.

'Oh, my dear, you must not say such things.
Mr. Hamilton has told me over and over again
that he does not know how he would have got
through that miserable time but for his cousin
Etta's kindness. She did everything for him,
and nursed Gladys in her illness. I am sure
she would have died but for Etta. Dear me,
Flossie looks restless. I do believe she hears
her master's step outside. Yes, Flossie—that
is his knock. But I wonder who he is

bringing in with him.' And Mrs. Maberley
straightened herself and smoothed the folds of
her satin gown, and tried to look as usual,
though there were tears in her bright eyes and
her hands were a little tremulous. I do not
know why I felt so sure that it would be Mr.
Hamilton, but I was not at all surprised when
he followed the tall old Colonel into the room.
But he certainly looked astonished when he
saw me.

'Miss Garston,' he ejaculated, darting one
of his keen looks at me. But when he had
shaken hands he sat down by Mrs. Maberley
somewhat silently.

I was rather sorry to see Mr. Hamilton, for
our talk had unsettled me and made me feel
nervous in his presence. I was afraid he would
read something from our faces. And I certainly
saw him look at me more than once, as though
something had aroused his suspicion. For the
first time I was unwilling to encounter one of
those straight glances. I felt guilty, as though
I must avoid his eyes, but all the more I felt
he was watching me.

I was anxious to put a stop to this uncomfortable state of things, but I could not silence

Mrs. Maberley, who was relating to her husband the story of poor Flossie's accident. My presence of mind and skill were so much lauded, and the Colonel said so many civil things, that I felt myself getting hotter every moment.

Mr. Hamilton came at last to my relief.

'I think Miss Garston resembles me in one thing, Colonel. She hates to be thanked for doing her duty. You will drive her away if you say any more about Flossie. Oh, I thought so,' as I stretched out my hand for my hat; 'I thought I interpreted that look aright. Well, I must be going, too. I only brought him back safe to you, Mrs. Maberley. By the bye, Colonel, I shall tell Gladys that you have never asked after her.'

'My sweetheart, Gladys! To be sure I have not. Well, how is she, my dear fellow?'

'As obstinate as ever, Colonel. Came downstairs to-day and declares she will go to early service to-morrow, because it will be Christmas Day, and she has never missed yet. Women are kittle cattle to manage. Now, Miss Garston, if you are ready I will see you a little on your way.'

I knew it was no good to remonstrate, so I

held my peace. Mrs. Maberley kissed me quite affectionately and begged me to come whenever I had an hour to spare.'

' I wish I had known you before, my dear. But there, we all make mistakes sometimes.' And she patted me on the shoulder. ' Edbrooke, will you see them out ? He will be your friend for ever, after your goodness to Flossie—won't you, Edbrooke ? '

I never felt so afraid of Mr. Hamilton before. I was wondering what I should say to him, and hoping that he had not noticed my nervousness, when he startled me excessively by saying—

' What makes you look so odd this evening ? You are not a bit yourself, Miss Garston. Come ! I shall expect you to confess. Mrs. Maberley is an old friend of mine, and I am very much attached to her. I should like to know what you and she have been talking about ? '

It was too dark for Mr. Hamilton to see my face, so I answered a little flippantly,

' I daresay you would like to know. Women are certainly not much more curious than men, after all.'

'Oh! as to that, I am not a bit curious,' was the contradictory answer. 'But, all the same, I intend to know. So you may as well make a clean breast of it.'

'But—but you have no right to be so inquisitive, Mr. Hamilton.'

'Again I say I am not inquisitive, but I mean to know this. Mrs. Maberley had been crying. I could see the tears in her eyes. You looked inclined to cry too, Miss Garston. Now' —after a moment's hesitation, as though he found speech rather difficult—' I know the dear old lady has only one fault. She is rather too fond of gossiping about her neighbours, though she does it in the kindest manner. May I ask if her talk this evening at all related to a family not a hundred miles away from Maplehurst?'

His voice sounded hard and satirical in the darkness. 'I wish you would not ask me such a question, Mr. Hamilton,' I returned much distressed. 'It was not my fault—I did not wish—— ;' but he interrupted me.

'Of course, I knew it. When am I ever deceived by a face or manner?—not by yours, certainly. So my good old friend told you

about that miserable affair; I wish she had
held her tongue a little longer—I wish——'

But I burst out full of remorse—

'Oh, Mr. Hamilton, I am so sorry; I have
no right to know, but indeed I was hardly to
blame.'

'Who says you are to blame?' he returned,
so harshly that I remained silent; 'it is no fault
of yours if people will not be silent. But all the
same, I am sorry that you know; your opinion
of me is quite changed now, eh? You think
me a hard-hearted taskmaster of a brother;
well, it does not matter—Gladys would have
made you believe that in time.'

His voice was so full of concentrated bitterness that I longed to say something consoling;
in his own fashion he had been kind to me, and
I did not wish to misjudge him.

'I know your sister Gladys sufficiently to
be sure that she will never act ungenerously by
her brother,' I returned hotly. 'Mr. Hamilton,
you need not say such things, it is not for me
to judge.'

'But, all the same, you will judge,' he
replied moodily. 'Oh! I know how you good
women cling together—you know nothing of a

man's nature—you cannot estimate his difficulties; because he has not got your sweet
nature, because he cannot bear insolence patiently—oh!' with an abruptness that was almost
rude but for the concealed pain in his voice,
'I am not going to excuse myself to you—why
should I? I have only to account to my Maker
and my own conscience,' and he was actually
walking off in the darkness, for we were now
in sight of the parlour window, but I called
him back so earnestly that he could not refuse
to obey.

'Mr. Hamilton, pray do not leave me like
this; it makes me unhappy. Do you know it
is Christmas Eve?'

'Well, what of that?' with a short laugh.

'People ought not to quarrel and be disagreeable to each other on Christmas Eve.'

'I am afraid, Miss Garston, that I do feel
intensely disagreeable this evening.'

'Yes, but you must try and forgive me
all the same. I could not quite help myself;
but indeed I do not mean to judge you or
any one, and I should like you to shake
hands.'

'There, then,' with a decidedly hearty

grasp; and then, without releasing me, 'so you don't think so very badly of me after all?'

'I am very sorry for you,' was my prudent answer; 'I think you have had a great deal to bear. Good-night Mr. Hamilton.'

'Wait a minute, you have not answered my question; you must not have it all your own way. I repeat, has Mrs. Maberley given you a very bad impression of my character?'

'Certainly not; oh, she spoke most kindly; I should not have been afraid if you had heard the whole of our conversation.'

'I wish I had heard it.'

'She made me feel very sorry for you all. Oh, what trouble there is in the world, Mr. Hamilton! It does seem so blind and foolish to sit in judgment on other people—how can we know their trials and temptations?'

'That is spoken like a sensible woman. Try to keep a good opinion of us, Miss Garston; we shall be the better for your friendship. Well, so we are friends again, and this little misunderstanding is healed; so much the better; I should hate to quarrel with you. Now run in out of the cold.'

I hastened to obey him, but he stood at the

gate until I had entered the house; his voice
and manner had quite changed during the last
few minutes, and had become strangely gentle,
reminding me of his sister Gladys' voice. What
a singular man he was!—and yet I felt sorry for
him.   I wonder if he is really to blame !' I
thought, as I opened the parlour door.

The lamp was alight, the fire burnt ruddily ;
Tinker was stretched on the rug as usual, but
something else was on the rug too.

A girlish figure in a dark tweed gown was
huddled up before the grate ; a head, with short
thick locks of hair tossing roughly on her neck,
turned quickly at my entrance.

' Jill ! '

' Yes, it is I, Ursie, dear ! Oh, you darling
Bear, what a time you have been!' Two strong
arms pulled me down in the usual fashion, a
hot cheek was pressed lovingly against mine.

' Oh, Jill, Jill, what does this mean ? ' I exclaimed in utter amazement; but for a long time
Jill only laughed and hugged me, and there
was no getting an answer to my question.

CHAPTER XXI.

'I RAN AWAY, THEN!'

'NOW, Jill,' I demanded at last, taking her by the shoulders, 'I insist on knowing what this means,' and when I spoke in that tone Jill always obeyed me at once.

So she shook her untidy mane, and looked at me with eyes that were brimful of fun and naughtiness.

'Very well, Ursie, dear, if you will know, you shall; but first sit down in that cosy-looking chair, and I will put my elbows in your lap, in the dear old fashion, and then we can talk nicely. What a snug little room this is! it looked just delicious when I came in, and Mrs. Barton made me such a nice cup of tea, and then I went upstairs to look at your bed-

room, and there was a beautiful fire there, and
Mrs. Barton says you always have one; so you
are not so poor and miserable, after all.'

'I am not at all poor, thank you; and I
work so hard that I think I deserve to be warm
and comfortable. And when people live alone,
a fire is a nice, cheerful companion. But this
is not answering my question, Jocelyn.'

Now Jill hated me to call her Jocelyn, so
she made a face at me, and said, in rather a
grumpy voice, 'Well, I ran away, then!'

'Ran away from Hyde Park Gate; were
you mad, Jill?'

'Oh dear no, not from Hyde Park Gate.
Did you not get my letter? Oh! I remember,
I forgot to post it; it is in my blotting-case
now. Then you did not know that Sara has
scarlatina?'

'No, indeed; but I am very sorry to hear
it.'

'Oh! she is nearly well now; but no one
knows how she caught it. There was a terrible
fuss when Dr. Armstrong pronounced it scarlatina. Mamma made father take lodgings at
Brighton at once, and Fräulein and I were
packed off there at a minute's notice. You

can fancy what my life has been for the last
ten days, mewed up in a dull, ugly parlour
with that old cat.'

'My poor, dear Jill; but why did you not
write to me, and I would have come over at
once?'

'So I did write, twice, and I do believe
that horrid creature never posted my letters—I
daresay they are in her pocket now—and I
could not get out by myself until to-day. Now
just think, Ursula, what sort of a Christmas
Day I was likely to have; and then you never
came to me, and I got desperate; so when
Fräulein said she had one of her headaches,'
and here Jill made a comical grimace, 'I just
made up my mind to take French leave, and
spend Christmas Day with you, and here I am:
and scold me, if you dare, and I will hug you
to death.' And, indeed, Jill's powerful young
arms were quite capable of fulfilling her
threat.

'It is not for me to scold you,' I replied
quietly, 'but I am afraid you will get into
trouble for this piece of recklessness. Think
how frightened poor Fräulein will be when she
misses you.'

'Poor Fräulein, indeed! a deceitful creature like that. Why, Ursula, what do you think? I just peeped into her room to be sure that she was safe, and it was all dark; she was not there at all. Oh, oh, my lady, I said to myself, so that is your little game, is it? And just to be certain I rang at the bell at 37 Brunswick Place, where the Schumackers live, and asked the servant if Fräulein Hennig was still there, and when I heard that she was having tea, I nearly laughed in his face. What do you think of that for an instructress of youth—getting up the excuse of a headache, and leaving me over those stupid lessons, while she paid a visit on her own account! Does she not deserve a thorough good fright as a punishment?'

'I think Aunt Philippa ought to be undeceived. I have never trusted Fräulein Hennig since you told me she shut herself up in her bedroom to read novels. Jill, my dear, you have acted very wrongly, and I am afraid we shall all get into trouble over this schoolgirl trick of yours. I must think what is best to be done under the circumstances.'

'You may think as much as you like,' returned Jill, obstinately, 'but I have come to spend my Christmas Day with you, and nothing will induce me to go back to Fräulein ; I shall murder her if I do. Now, Ursie, darling,' in a coaxing voice, ' do be nice, and make much of me. You don't think how delicious it is to see your face again—it is such a dear face, and I like it ever so much better than Sara's and Lesbia's.'

I was unable to reply to this flattering speech, for Jill suddenly put up her hand—I noticed it was a little inky—and said, ' Hark, there is some one coming up to the door ! ' and for the moment we both believed that it was Fräulein ; but to Jill's immense relief it was only Mr. Tudor, with a great bough of holly in his hand.

' We have just finished at the church, and I have brought you this, Miss Garston,' he began, and then he stopped, and said, ' Miss Jocelyn here ! ' in a tone of extreme surprise, and Jill got up rather awkwardly, and shook hands with him. I could see that she felt shy and uncomfortable. I was very pleased to see Mr. Tudor, for I knew he would help us in this emergency. Jill was such a child, in spite of her womanly proportions, that I was sure that her escapade would not seriously shock him ; he was young enough himself to have a fellow-feeling for her, and I was not wrong. Mr. Tudor looked decidedly amused when I told him Jill had taken French leave. He tried to look grave until I had finished, but the effort was too much for him, and he burst out laughing.

Jill, who was looking very sulky, was so charmed by his merriment that she began to laugh too, and we were all as cheerful as possible until I called them to order, and asked Mr. Tudor if he would send off a telegram at once.

'A telegram! Oh, Ursula!' and Jill's dimples disappeared like magic.

'My dear, Fräulein would not have a moment's sleep to-night if she did not know you were safe. Do not be afraid, Jill ; we will spend our Christmas Day together, in spite of all the Fräuleins in the world.' And then I wrote off the telegram, and a short note, and gave them to Mr. Tudor. The telegram was necessarily brief :—

'Jocelyn safe with me. Will not return until Thursday. Write to explain.'

The note was more explanatory.

I apologised profusely to Fräulein for her pupil's naughtiness, but begged her to say nothing to her mother, as I would communicate myself with Aunt Philippa and let her know what had happened. Under the circumstances I thought it better to keep Jocelyn with me over Christmas Day, until I heard from Aunt Philippa. But she might depend on my bringing her back myself.

'It is far too polite,' growled Jill, who had been reading the letter over my shoulder. 'How can you cringe so to that creature?'

'I consider it a masterpiece of diplomacy,' observed Mr. Tudor, as I handed it for his inspection. 'Civil words pay best in the long run, and you know it was very naughty to run away, Miss Jocelyn.'

'It was nothing of the kind,' returned Jill, rebelliously. 'And I would do it again to-morrow. I am more than sixteen; I am not a child now, and I have a right to come and see Ursula if I like.' And Jill threw back her head, and the colour came into her face, and she looked so handsome that I was not surprised to see Mr. Tudor regard her attentively.

I never saw a face so capable of varying expression as Jill's.

Jill declared she was glad when Mr. Tudor was gone. But I think she liked him very well on the whole—and, indeed, no one could dislike such a bright, kind-hearted fellow. As soon as he had left the house I had to call a council. It was quite certain my bed would not hold Jill, so at Mrs. Barton's suggestion some spare mattresses were dragged in my room and a bed made up on the floor. Jill voted this delicious; nothing could have pleased her more, and she was so talkative and excited that I had the greatest trouble in coaxing her to be quiet and let me go to sleep; in fact, I had to feign sleep to make her hold her tongue.

But I was much too restless to sleep, and once when I crept out of bed to replenish the fire I stood still for a moment to look at Jill.

She was sleeping as placidly as an infant in its cradle; her short black locks pushed back from her face, and one arm stretched on the coverlet. I was surprised to see how fine Jill's face really was. The ugly duckling, as Uncle

Brian called her, was fast changing into a swan. At present she was too big and undeveloped for grace ; her awkward manners and angularities made people think her rough and uncouth. ' I expect she will eclipse Sara's commonplace prettiness some day ; but, poor child, no one understands her,' I sighed, and as I tucked her up more warmly, with a kiss, Jill's sleepy arms found their way to my neck and held me there. ' Is not it delicious, Ursie, dear ? ' she murmured drowsily.

I was glad to see that Miss Hamilton was at the early service. She looked pale and delicate, but there was a brighter look upon her face when she nodded to me in the porch. Her brother was putting her into a fly, and Miss Darrell and Lady Betty followed.

I was rather surprised to see him close the door after them and step back into the porch. And the next moment he joined us.

' Well, Miss Garston,' holding out his hand, with a friendly smile, ' you see Gladys contrived to have her way. A happy Christmas to you ! But I see you are not alone,' looking rather inquisitively at Jill, who looked very big and shy as usual.

'I think you have heard of my cousin Jocelyn?' I returned, without entering into any further particulars. I should have been sorry for Jill's escapade to reach Mr. Hamilton's ears. But he shook hands with her at once, and said, very pleasantly, that he had heard of her from Mr. Cunliffe. And then, after a few more words, we parted.

Mr. Hamilton was unusually genial this morning. There was nothing in his manner to recall our stormy interview on the previous evening. Perhaps he wished to efface the recollection from my memory, for there was something significant in his smile, as though we perfectly understood each other.

I had laid awake for a long time thinking over Mrs. Maberley's talk and that uncomfortable walk from Maplehurst. Mr. Hamilton's voice and words haunted me ; the suppressed irritation and pain that almost mastered him, and how he had flung away from me in the darkness.

I was glad to remember that I had called him back and spoken a conciliatory word. No doubt he had been to blame. I could imagine him hard and bitter to a fault. But he had

suffered ; there were lines upon his face that
had been traced by no common experience.
No! it was not for me to judge him. As he
said, what could I know of a man's nature?
And I was still more glad when I saw Mr.
Hamilton in the church porch, and knew
that the day's harmony was not disturbed,
and that there was peace between us. His
bright, satisfied smile made me feel more
cheerful.

'What a strange-looking man!' observed
Jill, in rather a grumbling voice, as we walked
up the hill. 'Is that Mr. Hamilton? I thought
he was young ; but he is quite old, Ursula.'

' No, dear, not more than three or four and
thirty, Uncle Max says.'

' Well ! I call that old,' returned Jill, with
the obstinacy of sixteen. ' He is an old
bachelor too—for, of course, nobody wants to
marry him ; he is too ugly.'

'Oh, Jill, how absurd you are ! Mr.
Hamilton is not ugly at all. You will soon
get used to his face. It is only rather peculiar.'
And I quite meant what I said, for I had got
used to it myself.

' Humph ! ' observed Jill, significantly. But

she did not explain the meaning of her satirical smile, and I proceeded to call her attention to the hoar-frost that lay on the cottage roof, and the beauty of the clear winter sky. 'It is a glorious Christmas morning,' I finished.

We had a very merry breakfast, for Jill was almost wild with spirits, and then we went to church again. Gladys was in her usual place, and looked round at me with a smile as I entered. When the service was over, I went to the Marshalls' accompanied by Jill, who announced her intention of not letting me out of her sight, for I had to preside over the children's Christmas dinner, and to look after my patient. We visited Robin next, and then went on to the Lockes', and Jill sat open-eyed and breathless in a corner of the room as I sang carols to Phebe in the twilight.

She rose reluctantly when I put my hand on her shoulder and told her that we must hurry back to the cottage to make ourselves smart for the evening. Jill seldom troubled her head about such sublunary affairs as dress.

'I shall be obliged to wear my old tweed,' she said contentedly. 'I have only to smooth my hair, and then I shall be ready,' and she grumbled not a little when I insisted on arranging a beautiful spray of holly as a breast-knot, and twisting some very handsome coral beads that Charlie had given me round her neck. Jill always looked better for a touch of warm colour; the dark red berries just suited her brown skin. 'You will do better now,' I said, pushing her away gently, 'so you need not pout and hunch your shoulders. Have I not told you that it is your duty to make the best of yourself?—we cannot be all handsome, but we need not offend our neighbours' eyes,' but as usual Jill turned a deaf ear to my philosophy.

The study looked very cosy when we entered it, and Uncle Max gave us a warm welcome. To be sure he shook his head at Jill, and told her that he was afraid that she was a naughty girl, but both he and Mr. Tudor prudently refrained from teasing her on the subject of her escapade. On the contrary, they treated her with profound respect, as though she were a grown-up, sensible young lady, and this answered with Jill. She grew bright and animated, forgot her shyness, and talked in her quaint racy manner. I could see Mr. Tudor was much taken with her. She was so different to the stereotyped young lady, her cleverness and originality amused him, and I am sure Uncle Max was equally surprised and pleased.

I could see Max was making strenuous efforts to be cheerful, but every now and then he relapsed into gravity. After dinner I drew him aside a moment to speak to him about Jill; to my relief he promised to be a bearer of a letter to Aunt Philippa.

'I want to go up to town for a day or two,' he said, 'and I may as well do this business for you. How happy the child looks, Ursula; I wish you could keep her a little longer, she is very much improved. I had no idea that there was so much in her; she will be far more attractive than Sara when she has developed a moderate amount of vanity.' And I fully endorsed this opinion.

We went home early, for I could see Max was very tired, but both he and Mr. Tudor insisted on escorting us. It was a beautiful starlight night, clear and frosty, our footsteps rang crisply on the ground, not a breath of wind stirred the skeleton branches that stretched above our heads, a solemn peacefulness seemed to close us round. Jill's mirthful laugh quite

H 2

startled the echoes. She and Mr. Tudor were following very slowly. Once or twice we stood still and waited for them, but Mr. Tudor was in the middle of some amusing story and so they took no notice of us.

I told Max about my visit to Mrs. Maberley, and of the conversation that had taken place between us. 1 thought he started a little when I mentioned Eric Hamilton's name.

'What a pity,' he said quietly. 'I had hoped she would have told you herself. I was waiting for her to do so.'

'But Max, surely you might have told me!'

'Who—I—I should not have presumed. You must remember that I was in Hamilton's confidence—and,' after a moment's hesitation, 'in hers too. Ursula,' with a sudden passionate inflexion in his voice, 'you have no idea how she loved that poor boy, and how she suffered —it nearly killed her. Now you know why I say that she is lonely and wants a friend.'

'But she has you, Max,' I exclaimed involuntarily, for I knew what he must have been to them in their trouble; Max could be as tender as a woman; but he started aside as though I had struck him; and his voice was quite changed as he answered me.

'You mistake, Ursula. I was only her clergyman; if she confided in me it was because she could not do otherwise; she is naturally reserved. She would find it easier to be open with you.'

'I do not think so, Max. I—but what does it matter what I think! There is one question I want to ask : do you think Mr. Hamilton was at all to blame?'

'I am Hamilton's friend,' he returned, in a tone that made me regret that I had asked the question, and then he stood still and waited for the others to join us. Indeed he did not speak again, except to wish us good-night.

'It is the loveliest Christmas Day I have ever spent,' cried Jill, flinging herself on me, and she was no light weight. 'I do like Mr. Tudor so; he is nicer than any one I know, more like a nice funny boy than a man, only he tells me he can be grave sometimes. What was the matter with Mr. Cunliffe?—he looks tired and worried and not inclined to laugh.' And so Jill chattered on without waiting for my answers, talking in the very fulness of her young heart, until I pretended again to be asleep, and then she consented to be quiet.

I saw Max for a few minutes the next day when he came to fetch my letter. He looked more like himself, only there was still a tired expression about his eyes; but he talked very cheerfully of what he should do during the few days he intended to remain in town.

I made him promise to be very diplomatic with Aunt Philippa, and he most certainly kept his word, for the next morning I received a letter that surprised us both, and that drove Jill nearly frantic with joy.

Aunt Philippa's letter was very long and rambling. She began by expressing herself deeply shocked and grieved at Jocelyn's behaviour, which was both dishonourable and un-ladylike, and had given her father great pain. 'Dear old dad! I don't believe it,' observed Jill, pursing her lips at this.

Aunt Philippa regretted that she could no longer trust her young daugher—she was sure Sara would never have behaved so at her age —and she felt much wounded by Jocelyn's defiant action. At the same time she was equally deceived in Fräulein Hennig; she was certainly

more to blame than Jocelyn. Mr. Cunliffe had
told her things that greatly surprised her.
Uncle Brian was very angry, and insisted that
she should be dismissed. Under these distressing circumstances, and as it would not be safe
for Jocelyn to come back to Hyde Park Gate
until the rooms had been properly disinfected,
she must beg me as a favour to herself and
Uncle Brian to keep Jocelyn with me until
they went to Hastings. Mr. Cunliffe knew of a
finishing governess, a Miss Gillespie, who was
most highly recommended as a well-principled
and thoroughly cultured person, only she
would not be at liberty for three or four weeks,
—as I reached this point of Aunt Philippa's
letter, I was obliged to lay it down to prevent
myself from being strangled.

'Well, Jill, there is no need to hug me to
death; it is Uncle Max that you have to thank,
and not me.'

'Yes, but you see it would never do to hug
him, for he is not a bit my uncle, so I am
doing it by deputy,' observed Jill, recklessly.
'Oh, Ursula, what a darling you are! and what
a dear fellow he is!—to think of my staying
here three or four weeks—you will let me

help you nurse people, won't you?' very
coaxingly.

'We will see about that presently; but,
Jill, you have never opened your mother's
letter. Now, as it is perfectly impossible that
you can sleep on the floor for weeks, and as I
do not intend to keep such a chatterbox in my
room, I am going to see what Mrs. Barton
advises.' And leaving Jill to digest Aunt
Philippa's scolding as well as she could, I
went in search of the little widow.

I found to my relief that there was another
room in the cottage, though it could not boast
of much furniture beyond a bed and washstand;
so, after a little consideration, I started off to
the Vicarage to hold a consultation with Mrs.
Drabble.

The upshot of our talk was so satisfactory,
and Mrs. Barton and Nathaniel worked so well
in my service, that when bedtime came Jill
found herself the possessor of quite a snug
room. There were curtains up at the window
and strips of carpet on the floor, a dressing-
table had been improvised out of a deal pack-
ing-case, and covered with clean dimity. Jill's
travelling-box stood in one corner, and on the

wall there was a row of neat pegs for Jill's
dresses. Jill exclaimed at the clean trim look of
the room, but I am sure she regretted her bed
on the floor. She came down presently in her
scarlet dressing-gown to give me a final hug
and reiterate her petition for work.

'Mamma has talked a lot of rubbish about
my keeping up my studies and practising two
hours a day, and she means to disinfect my
books and send them down, but I have made
up my mind that I will not open one. I am
going to enjoy myself and nurse sick people,
and do real work, instead of grinding away at
that stupid German;' and Jill set her little white
teeth, and looked determined, so I thought it
best not to contradict her.

'I am so glad Uncle Max thought of Miss
Gillespie, dear.'

'Who is she? I hate her already; I expect
she is only an Anglicised Fräulein,' observed
Jill, with a vixenish look.

'You are quite wrong. Miss Gillespie is
Scotch, and she is very nice and good, and
pretty too, for I have often heard Uncle Max
talk of her. Her father was Max's great
friend, and at his death the daughters were

obliged to go out in the world ; Miss Gillespie
is the eldest. No, she is not very young—
nearly forty, I believe—but she is so nice-
looking ; she was engaged to a clergyman, but
he died, and they had been engaged so many
years, and so now she will not marry. She is
very cheerful, however, and all her pupils love
her, and I am sure you will be happy with
her, Jill.'

Jill would not quite allow this, but the
next day she recurred to the subject, and
asked me a good many questions about Miss
Gillespie, and when I told her that it was
settled that Miss Gillespie should join them
at Hastings, she really looked quite pleased,
but nothing would induce her to open the
case of books Aunt Philippa had sent down,
and when I told Uncle Max he only laughed.

' Let her be as idle as she likes, she is over-
educated now, and knows far more than most
girls of her age. Take her about with you, and
make her useful.' And I followed this advice
implicitly, but for a different reason—there was
no keeping Mr. Tudor out of the house, so
when I was engaged, and Jill could not be
with me, I took advantage of a general invita-

tion that Miss Hamilton had given me, and sent her up to Gladwyn.

They were all very kind to her, and she seemed to amuse Miss Darrell, but after a time Mr. Tudor began going there too, and then indeed I should have been at my wits' end, only Mrs. Maberley came to my rescue. She took a fancy to Jill, and Jill reciprocated it, and presently she and Lady Betty began to spend most of their idle hours at Maplehurst.

CHAPTER XXII.

'THEY HAVE BLACKENED HIS MEMORY FALSELY.'

LOVED having Jill with me, but I could not deny to myself or other people that I found her a great responsibility. In the first place I had so little leisure to devote to her, for just after Christmas I was unusually busy. Poor Mrs. Marshall died on the eve of the new year, and both Mr. Hamilton and I feared that Elspeth would soon follow her.

A hard frost had set in, and Grannie's feeble strength seemed to succumb under the pressure of the severe cold; she had taken to her bed, and lay there growing weaker every day. Poor Mary had died very peacefully, with her hand in her husband's. I had been with her all day, and I did not leave until it was all over.

Jill was as good as gold, and helped me with Elspeth and the children, and she always spent an hour or two with Robin ; but by-and-by she began asking to go up to Gladwyn of her own accord, or proposing to have tea with Mrs. Maberley.

' Of course I would prefer to stop with you, Ursie dear,' she said affectionately. ' I would rather talk to you than to any one else ; but then, you see, you are never at home, and when you do come in, poor darling, you are so tired that you are only fit for a nap,' and I could not deny that this was the truth. After my hard day's work I was not always disposed for Jill's lively chatter, and yet her bright face was a very pleasant sight for tired eyes.

I used to question her sometimes about her visits to Gladwyn, and she was always ready to talk of what had passed in the day. She and Lady Betty had struck up quite a friendship ; this rather surprised me, as they were utterly dissimilar, and had different tastes and pursuits. Jill was so far superior in intelligence and intellectual power ; she had wider sympathics too; and though Lady Betty had a fund of originality, and was fresh and naïve, I could hardly understand Jill's fancy for her, until Jill said one day:

'I do like that dear Lady Betty, she is such a crisp little piece of human goods; no one has properly unfolded her, or tested her good qualities; she is quite new and fresh, a novelty in girls. One never knows what she will say or do next—it is that that fascinates me, I believe; because,' went on Jill, and her great eyes grew bright and puzzled, 'it is not that she is clever—one gets to the bottom of her at once; there is not enough depth to drown you.'

Jill did not take so readily to Gladys; she admired her, even liked her, but frankly owned that she found her depressing—'if I talk to her long, I get a sort of ache over me,' she observed in her graphic way. 'It is not that she looks dreadfully unhappy, but that there is no happiness in her face. Do you know what I mean, for I am apt to be vague?—it rests me to look at you, Ursula, there is something quiet and comfortable in your expression; now Miss Hamilton looks as though she had lost some-

thing she values, or never had it, and must go
on looking for it like that poor ghost lady
who wanted to find her lost pearl.'

Jill never could be induced to say much in
Mr. Hamilton's favour, though he was very
civil to her and paid her a great deal of attention. 'Oh, him,' she would say contemp-
tuously, if I ever hazarded an observation,
'I never take much notice of odd-looking, ugly
men—they may be clever, but they are not in
my line. Mr. Hamilton stares too much for
my taste, and I don't believe he is kind to his
sisters; they are half afraid of him,' and
nothing would induce her to alter her opinion.

But Miss Darrell thoroughly amused her.
Jill's shrewd, honest eyes were hardly in fault
there; she used to narrate with glee any little
fact she could glean about 'the lady with two
faces,' as she used to call her.

'Oh, she is a deep one,' Jill would say. 'I
could not understand her at first. I thought
she was just bright, and talkative, and good-
natured, and I thought it nice to sit and listen
to her, and she was very kind and petted me
a good deal, and I did not find her out at
first.'

'Find her out; what do you mean, Jill?' I asked innocently.

'Why, that she is not good-natured a bit, really,' with a sagacious nod of her head; 'she keeps a stock of smiles for cousin Giles and any chance visitor. She is not half so nice and charming when Miss Hamilton and Lady Betty are alone with her—oh, I heard her one day, when I was in the conservatory with Lady Betty. Lady Betty held up her finger and said "Hush!" and there she was talking in such a disagreeable, sneering voice to Miss Hamilton, only I stopped my ears and would not listen. And now she has got used to me she says unpleasant little things before my face, and then when "dear cousin Giles comes in"'—and here Jill looked wicked—'she is all sweetness and amiability, quite charming, in fact. Now that is what I hate, for a person to wear two faces, and have different voices— it shows they are not true.'

'Well, perhaps you are right, dear,' for, without being uncharitable to Miss Darrell, I wished to put Jill on her guard a little.

'I don't like the way she talks about you,' went on Jill, indignantly. 'She always begins when we are alone; not exactly saying things so much as implying them.'

'Indeed, what sort of things?' I asked carelessly.

'Oh, she is always hinting that it is rather odd for you to be living alone; she calls you deliciously unconventional and strong-minded, but I know what she means by that. Then she is so curious, she is always trying to find out how often Mr. Cunliffe or Mr. Tudor comes to see you, or if you go to the Vicarage; and she said one day that she thought you preferred gentlemen's society to ladies, as they could never induce you to come up to Gladwyn, but of course you saw plenty of her cousin Giles in the village.'

I felt my cheeks burn at this unwarrantable accusation, but Jill begged me not to disturb myself.

'She won't make those sort of speeches to me again,' she said calmly. 'She had a piece of my mind then that will last her for a long time.'

'I hope you were not rude, Jill?'

Oh, no! I only flew into a passion, and asked her how she dared to imply such a thing, that my cousin Ursula was the best and the dearest woman in the world, and that no one else could hold a candle to her. " Ursula care for gentlemen's society," I exclaimed, " why at Hyde Park Gate we never could get her to remain in the drawing-room when those stupid officers were there—she never would talk to any of them, except old Colonel Trevanion, who is nearly blind! You do not understand Ursula; she is a perfect saint, she is the simplest, most unselfish, grandest-hearted creature; and you make out that she is a silly flirt like Sara," and then I had to hold my tongue, though I was as red as a turkey-cock, for there was Mr. Hamilton staring at us both, and asking if I were in my senses, and why I was quarrelling about my cousin, for of course my voice was as gruff and cross as possible.'

' Oh, Jill!' I exclaimed, much distressed, ' how could you say such absurd things?—you know I never like you to talk in this exaggerated fashion. A saint indeed, a pretty sort of saint Mr. Hamilton must think me,' for it nettled me to think that he had ever heard Jill's ridiculous nonsense.

' Wait a moment till I have finished—you are not too saintly to be cross sometimes. I

will tell him that if you like. Well, when he
said this about quarrelling, Miss Darrell gave
him one of her sweet smiles.

‘ “ Nonsense, Giles, as though I mind what
this dear foolish child says; she is indulging
in a panegyric on her cousin's virtues, because
I said she was a little masculine and strong-
minded, and rather looked down upon us poor
women. I have pressed her over and over
again to spend an evening with us, but she
always puts us off. I am afraid we Gladwyn
ladies are not to her taste.”

‘ “ Don't be silly, Etta, have I not told you
poor old Elspeth is dying?—Miss Garston will
not leave her, you may be sure of that,” and
then Mr. Hamilton said to me in quite a nice
way—oh, I did not dislike him so much that
evening—“I daresay you misunderstand Etta.
I assure you we all think most highly of
your cousin, and she will always be a welcome
guest here, and I hope you will induce her to
come soon.” Wasn't it nice of him? dear Etta
did not dare to say another word.’

‘Very nice, Jill, but indeed I do not want
to hear any more of Miss Darrell's speeches,’
and I got up hastily and opened the piano to

put a stop to the conversation. Jill was always pleased when I would sing to her, but somehow my voice was not quite in order that evening.

The next day Jill surprised me very much by asking me if I knew that Miss Hamilton was going to Bournemouth for the rest of the winter.

'Mrs. Maberley has invited her, and Mr. Hamilton thinks it will do her so much good; they are going early next week. She wants to see you, Ursula; she says you have not met since Christmas—could you go this afternoon? Miss Darrell will be out.'

I considered for a moment, and then said yes, I would certainly go up to Gladwyn. It made me feel a little dull to think Miss Hamilton was going away; we had not ex-changed a word since that Sunday evening, but I had thought of her so much since then. My patients had engrossed my time, but hardly my thoughts; poor Elspeth was slowly dying, and I had to be constantly with her. Marshall had not yet resumed work, but he was in poor spirits from the loss of his wife, and could hardly be a comfort to the poor creature. I put off my visit to Phebe until the evening, and

walked up to Gladwyn with Jill; she and Lady
Betty were going for a walk, and were to
have tea with the Maberleys. I learnt afterwards that Mr. Tudor met them quite accidentally about three miles from Heathfield, and
had accompanied them to Maplehurst, where
he made himself so pleasant to the old lady
that he was pressed to remain. Oh, Mr. Tudor,
I am afraid you are not quite so artless as you
look! I began to wish Aunt Philippa would
soon recall Jill.

I found Miss Hamilton alone, and she
seemed very glad to see me; her fair face quite
flushed with pleasure when she saw me enter
the drawing-room.

'I was afraid it was some stupid visitor,'
she said frankly, ' when I heard the door-bell
ring. Did it trouble you to come?—how tired
you look; there, you shall take Giles's chair,'
putting me with gentle force in a big blue-
velvet chair that always stood by the fire; and
then she took off my wraps and unfastened
my gloves, and made me feel how glad she
was to wait on me.

'You are going away,' I said rather
lugubriously, for I felt all at once how I should

miss her. She looked a little better and brighter, I thought, or was it only temporary excitement?

'Yes,' she returned seriously, but not sadly, 'I think it will be better. I am almost glad to go away, except that I shall not see you,' looking at me affectionately.

'Oh, if you wish to go,' for I was so relieved to hear her say this.

'It is not that I wish it exactly, but that I feel it will be better—things are so uncomfortable just now, more than usual I think. Etta seems always worrying herself and me; sometimes I fancy that she wants to get rid of me, that I am too troublesome,' with a faint smile. 'She worries about my health and want of spirits. I suppose I am rather a depressing element in the house, and as I get rather tired of all this fuss, I think it will be better to leave it behind for a little.'

'That sounds as though you were driven away from home, Miss Hamilton.'

'Miss Hamilton,' reproachfully; 'that is naughty, Ursula. I do not call you Miss Garston.'

'Gladys, then.'

'Perhaps my restlessness is driving me away,' she returned sadly. 'I do feel so restless without my work. I never minded Etta's fussiness so much. I daresay she means it kindly, but it harasses me. I am one of those reserved people who do not find it easy to talk of their feelings, bodily or mental, except to a chosen few. You are one, perhaps not the only one.'

'Of course not,' for she hesitated. 'You do not suppose that I laid such flattering unction to my soul.'

'Oh, but I could tell you anything,' she returned seriously. 'You seem to draw out one's thoughts while one is thinking them. Yes, I am sorry to leave you even for a few weeks ; but for many reasons Giles is right, and the change will be good for me.'

'If you will only come back looking better and brighter I will gladly let you go.'

'I do not promise you that,' she answered quickly, 'unless you remove the pressure of a very heavy burthen ; but I shall be quieter and more at peace, and I am very fond of Colonel and Mrs. Maberley—they are dear people, and they spoil me dreadfully.'

'I am thankful some one spoils you, Gladys.'

She smiled at that.

'Uncle Max is still away,' I observed, after a brief silence. 'He went to Torquay to see an invalid friend, and he is still there. Mr. Tudor does not expect him back until the end of next week.'

'Yes, I know,' she returned, in a low voice, 'but we shall be at Bournemouth before then. Will you bid him good-bye for me, Ursula, and say that I hope his visit has rested and refreshed him; he was not very well, you told me.'

'No, but he is better now; he writes very cheerfully. Gladys, when you come back you will be stronger, I hope. I really do hope you will resume your work then; it will be far better for you to do so.'

'You cannot judge,' she said gently. 'I am afraid that I shall be unable to do that,' and somehow her manner closed the subject; but I was determined to make her speak on another subject.

'I want to tell you something that I think you ought to know.' I began rather abruptly. 'Mrs. Maberley spoke to me about your brother Eric.'

' Ursula ! '

' I could not let you go away and not know this—it did not seem honest; it has troubled me a great deal. Mrs. Maberley would tell me, and she told it so nicely ; and Mr. Hamilton is aware that I know, and I am afraid he is not pleased about it.'

She put up her hands to her face for a moment, with a gesture full of distress.

' I meant to tell you myself,' she said in a stifled voice, ' but not now—not until I felt stronger.'

' And now you will not have that pain, Gladys. I think you ought to be relieved that some one else has told me.' But she shook her head.

' How do I know what they said? And Giles is aware of it, you say. Oh, Ursula, for pity's sake, tell me, has he talked to you about Eric ? '

' No, no, not in the way you mean ; he only said that we must not judge or misjudge other people. He seemed afraid that I should mis-judge him.'

' Oh, I am thankful to know that. I could not bear to have the poor boy discussed between you two. Giles would have made you believe everything, he has such a way with him, and you would not know any better. Oh, Ursula,' in a piteous voice, 'you must not listen to them—they are all so hard on my poor darling. Faulty as he was, he was innocent of the crime laid to his charge; they have accused him falsely. Eric never took that cheque.'

I could see she was strongly agitated. Her delicate throat swelled with emotion, and she took hold of my hands and held them tightly, and her large blue-grey eyes were fixed on my face with such a beseeching expression that I could have promised to believe anything—and yet she was right. Mr. Hamilton had a way with him that influenced people strongly; he could speak with a power and authority that seemed to dominate one in spite of oneself. It has always appeared to me that we poor women are easily silenced and subjugated by a strong masculine will. It is difficult to assert a timid individuality in the presence of a regnant force.

I answered her as gently as I could. 'Dear Gladys, you will make yourself ill. Will it give you any relief to speak out? I will listen to anything you have to say.'

She drew a deep breath, and the colour ebbed back into her face.

'Perhaps it may be a relief; I am weary of silence—of trying to bear it alone—and other things are wearing me out. Etta is not so far wrong, after all,' and then she stopped, and looked at me wistfully, and her lips trembled. 'Ursula, you are a nurse; you go about comforting sick bodies and sick minds. If I am ill—one must be ill sometimes—will you promise to come and take care of me, in spite of all Etta may do or say?'

I hesitated for a moment, for it seemed to me impossible to give an unconditional promise, but she continued reproachfully, 'You cannot have the heart to refuse. I wanted to ask you this before. You would not, surely, leave me to eat out my heart in this loneliness! If you knew what it is to have Etta with one at such times—an east wind would be more merciful and comforting. I know I am expressing myself far too strongly, but all this excites me. Do promise me this, Ursula. Giles will not hinder you coming—he appreciates you thoroughly—it will only be Etta who may try to oppose you.'

Gladys was right; I had not the heart to refuse, so I gave her the required promise, and she grew calmed at once.

'Now that is settled I can breathe more freely,' she said presently. 'I am afraid I am growing fanciful, but lately I have had such a horror of being ill. Giles would be kind, I know—he is always kind in illness; but he lets Etta influence him. Ursula, she influenced him and turned him against my poor boy; with all Giles's faults—and he can be very hard and stern and unforgiving—I am sure that of his own acccord he would never have been so harsh to Eric.'

'But Mrs. Maberley told me that Miss Darrell took your brother Eric's part.'

'Yes, I know, she believes in Etta, and so does Giles; but she is not true; she has a dangerous way of implying blame when she is apparently praising a person—have you never noticed this? Giles was always more angry with Eric after Etta had been into the study to intercede for him. If she would only have let him alone; but that is not Etta's way, she must make or mar people's lives.'

There was a concentrated bitterness in Gladys' voice, and her face grew stern.

' There was no love between them. Eric detested Etta, and on her side I know she disliked him. Eric never would tell me the reason ; he was always hinting that he had found her out, and that she knew it, and that in consequence she wanted to get rid of him ; but I thought it was all fancy on the poor boy's part, and I used to laugh at him. I wish I had not laughed now, for there was doubtless truth in what he said.'

' You were very fond of him, Gladys ? ' I asked softly, and as I spoke her face changed, and its expression grew soft and loving in a moment.

' Love him ! he was everything to me, he was my twin, you know—and so beautiful. Oh ! I never saw a man's face so beautiful as his ; he had such bright ways too, and such a ringing laugh—I wake up sometimes and fancy I hear it—and then came his whistle and light footstep springing up the stairs, but it is only a part of my dream.' She sighed and went on.

'He was so fond of me, and used to tell me everything, and he was never cross to me however put out and miserable he was; and I know they made him very miserable. Giles was so strict with him, and would not give him any liberty, and when Eric rebelled he was cruel to him.'

'Oh, not cruel, surely.' I could not help the involuntary exclamation. I thought Gladys looked at me a little strangely before she answered.

'It seemed cruel to us; he was very harsh, oh, terribly harsh; but I think—nay, I am sure he has repented of his hardness. I was slow to forgive him; perhaps it would be more true to say I have not wholly forgiven him yet; but I know now that he has suffered, that he would undo a great deal of the past if he could, and this makes me more merciful. Sometimes in my heart I feel quite sorry for Giles.'

CHAPTER XXIII.

THE MYSTERY AT GLADWYN.

JUST then Leah entered the room to replenish the fire, and Gladys dropped my hand hastily and took up a screen.

'When my brother comes in we will have tea, Leah,' she said quickly. 'Where is Thornton that he does not come in to do this?'

'I was passing through the hall and I thought I would have a look at the fire, ma'am,' observed Leah, as she stooped to throw on a log. As she did so, I saw her take a furtive look at us both—it gave me an unpleasant feeling, and a moment afterwards she said in a soft civil voice,

'There is no reason why Thornton should not bring tea now, if you like, ma'am. Master never cares to be waited for, and most likely he will be late this afternoon. I can walk home with Miss Garston when she is ready. I am sure my mistress would spare me.'

'We will see about that presently, Leah; when I want Thornton I will ring for him.' Gladys spoke somewhat haughtily, and Leah left the room without another word; but I was sorry and troubled in my very heart to see Gladys motion me to be silent, and then go quickly to the door and open it, and stand there for a moment. Her colour was a little heightened when she came back to her seat.

'She has gone now, but we must be careful and not speak loudly. I hate myself for being so suspicious, but I have found out that some of our conversations have been retailed to Etta. I am afraid Leah listens at the door—she came in just now to interrupt our talk; it is Thornton's place to put coals on the drawing-room fire.'

I felt an uncomfortable sensation creeping over me.

'Do you think she even heard us just now?'

'I fear so, and now Etta will know we have

been talking about Eric. Oh! I am glad I am going away, it gets too unbearable. Ursula, I shall write to you, and you must answer me. Think what a comfort your letters will be to me—I shall be able to depend on what you say. Lady Betty is so careless, she knows what Etta is, and yet she will leave her letters about, and more than once they have not reached me. I am afraid that Leah is a little unscrupulous in such matters.'

I was aghast as I listened to her, but she changed the subject quickly.

'What were we talking about? Oh, I said Giles was hard—and so he was; but Eric was faulty too.

'He was very idle, he would not work, and he thought of nothing but his painting. Giles always says I encouraged him in his idleness; but this is hardly the truth. I used to try and coax him to open his books, but he had got this craze for painting, and he spent hours at his easel. I thought it was a great pity that Giles forced him to take up law; if he had talent it was surely better for him to be an artist; but Giles and Etta persisted in ignoring his talent. They called his pictures daubs, and ridiculed his artistic notions.'

'Do you really believe that he would have worked successfully as an artist?'

'It is difficult for me to judge. Eric was so young, and had had little training, and then he only painted in a desultory way—as I have told you, he was very idle. I think if Giles had been more fatherly with him, and had remonstrated with him more gently, and showed him the sense and fitness of things, Eric would have been reasonable; but Etta made so much mischief between them, that things only got worse and worse. Eric was extravagant, he never managed money well, and he got into debt, and that made Giles furious, and when Eric lost his temper—for he was very hot and soon got into a passion—Giles's coolness and hard sneering speeches nearly drove Eric wild. He came to me one day in the garden looking as white as a sheet—that was the day before the cheque was missed—and told me in a conscience-stricken voice that it was all up between him and Giles, he had got into a passion and struck Giles across the face.'

'"I don't know why he did not knock me

down," cried the poor lad. " I deserved it, for I saw him wince with the pain ; but he only took me by the shoulder—you know how strong Giles is—and turned me out of the room without saying a word, and there was the mark of my hand across his cheek. I feel like Cain, I do indeed, Gladys—' For he that hateth his brother is a murderer,' and I hate Giles " ; and the poor boy—he was only twenty, Ursula— put his head down on my shoulder and sobbed like a child—if only Giles could have seen him then ! '

' Do you know what passed between them ? '

' Yes, I heard a little from both of them. Some of Eric's bills had been opened accidentally by Giles. Etta had told Giles that they were his, and he had called Eric to account. And then it seems that Eric's affairs were mixed up with another young man's, Edgar Brown, a very wild young fellow, with whom Giles had forbidden Eric to associate. They had been schoolfellows, and Giles knew his father, Dr. Brown, and disliked him much ; and it seems that Eric had promised to break with him, and had not kept his promise ; and when

Giles called him mean and dishonourable, Eric had forgotten himself, and struck Giles.

'"It is all over between us, I tell you, Gladys," the poor boy kept saying. "Giles says he shall take me away from Oxford, and I am to be put in an attorney's office; he declares I shall ruin him. I cannot stop here to be tormented and bullied, and I will never go near old Armstrong—why, the life would be worse than a convict's. I shall just go and enlist, and then there is a chance of getting rid of this miserable life." But I did not take much notice of this speech, for I knew Eric had no wish to enter the army; and certainly he would never do such a rash thing as enlist, he always declared he would as soon be a shoeblack. What does that look mean, Ursula?' for I was glancing uneasily at the door. Was it my fancy, or did I really hear the faint rustle of a dress on the tesselated pavement of the hall! In another moment Gladys understood, and her voice dropped into a whisper.

' Come closer to me, I mean to tell you all, in spite of them. I will be as quick as I can, or Giles will be here.

' I never saw Eric in such a state as he was

that day, he seemed nearly beside himself—
nothing I could say seemed to give him any
comfort. He shut himself up in his room
and refused to eat. He would not admit me
for a long time, but when he at last opened
the door, I saw that his table was strewn with
papers and a letter directed to Giles lay beside
them.

'We sat down and had a long talk. He told
me that he had got into more difficulties than
even Giles suspected. He had been led away by
Edgar Brown. I brought him all the money
I had, which was little enough, and promised
him my next quarter's allowance. I remember
he spoke again of enlisting, and said that any
life, however hard, would be preferable to the
present one. He could not stay here and be
slandered by Etta and bullied by Giles. He
seemed very unhappy, and once he put down
his head upon his arms and groaned. It was
just then that I heard a slight movement
outside the door, and opened it just in time
to see Leah gliding round the corner. Ursula,
she had heard every word that my poor boy
had said, and it is Leah's evidence that has
helped to criminate him.'

'Yes, I see; but did you not put your brother on his guard?'

'No,' she returned sadly, 'I made the grievous mistake of keeping Leah's eaves-dropping to myself. I thought Eric had enough to trouble him without adding to his discomfort. I would give much now to have done otherwise.

'I stayed up late with him, and did not leave him until he had promised to go to bed. Giles was still in the study when I went to my room, but he came up shortly afterwards, for I could hear his footsteps distinctly passing my door. He must have passed Leah in the passage, for I heard him say, "You are up late to-night, Leah," but her answer escaped me.

'I can tell you no more on my own evidence; but Eric's account, which I believe as surely as I am holding your hand now, is this:—

'He heard Giles come up to bed, and a sudden impulse prompted him to go down to the study and place his letter on Giles's desk. It was a very wild, foolish letter, written under strong excitement. I saw it afterwards, and felt that it had better not have been written. Among other things he informed

Giles that he would sooner destroy himself than go into Armstrong's office, and that he (Giles) had made his life so bitter to him that he thought he might as well do it—oh! Ursula, of course it was wrong of him, but, indeed, he had had terrible provocation. He had made up his mind to put this letter on Giles's desk before he slept; so he slipped off his boots that I might not hear him pass my door, and crept down to the study. He had his chamber candlestick, as he feared that he might have some difficulty with the fastenings, for he had heard Giles put up the chain and bell. All our doors on that floor have chains and bells; it is one of Giles's fads. To his great surprise the door was ajar, and when he put down the candle on the table, he had a passing fancy that the thick curtains that were drawn over one of the windows moved slightly, as though from a draught of air. He blamed himself afterwards that he had not gone up to the window and examined it, but in his perturbed mood he did not take much notice; but he was certainly startled when he turned round to see Leah, in her dark dressing-gown, standing in the threshold watching him with a queer look in her eyes. There was something in her expression that made him feel uneasy.

' " I thought it was thieves," she said, and now she looked not at him, but across at the curtain. " What are you doing with Master's papers, Mr. Eric ? "

' " Mind your own business," returned Eric, sulkily ; " do you think I am going to account to you for my actions? " and he took up his candlestick and marched off.

' And he left that woman in possession ? '

' Yes,' returned Gladys, in a peculiar tone, and then she hurried on : ' The next morning Giles missed a cheque for a large amount that he had received the previous night and placed in one of the compartments of his desk, and in its place he found Eric's letter. Do you notice the discrepancy here? Eric vowed to me that he had placed the letter on the desk, that he never dreamt of opening it, that he always believed Giles kept it locked, that if Giles had been careless and left the key in it he knew nothing about it. His business to the study was to put his letter where Giles would be likely to find it on entering the room. Ursula, how did that letter get into the desk?

'We were all summoned to the study when the cheque was missed. Etta fetched me. She said very little, and looked unusually pale. Giles was in a terrible state of anger, she informed me, and Leah was speaking to him.

'Alas! she had been speaking to some purpose. I found Eric almost dumb with fury. Giles had refused to believe his assertion of innocence, and he had no proof. Leah's statement had been overwhelming, and bore the outward stamp of veracity.

'She told her master that, thinking she heard a noise, and being fearful of thieves, she had crept down in her dressing-gown to the study, and to her horror had seen Mr. Eric with his hand in his brother's desk, and she could take her oath that he put some paper or other in his pocket. She had not liked to disturb her master, not knowing that there was money in the case.

'Ursula, I cannot tell you any more that passed. That woman had effectually blackened my poor boy's honour. No one believed his word, though he swore that he was innocent. I heard high words pass between the brothers. I know Giles called Eric a liar and a thief, and

Eric rushed at him like a madman, and then I fainted. When I recovered I found Lady Betty crying over me and Leah rubbing my hands. No one else was there. Eric had dashed up to his room, and Giles and Etta were in the drawing-room. I told Leah to go out of my sight, for I hated her; and I felt I did hate her. And when she left us alone I managed, with Lady Betty's help, to crawl up to Eric's room. But though we heard him raging about it he would not admit us. So I went and laid down on my bed and slept from sheer grief and exhaustion.

'When I woke from that stupor—for it was more stupor than sleep—it was late in the afternoon. I shall always believe the wine Leah gave me was drugged. How I wish I had dashed the glass away from my lips! But I was weak, and she had compelled me to drink it.

'Lady Betty was still sitting by me. She seemed half frightened by my long sleep. She said Eric had come in and had kissed me, but very lightly, so as not to disturb me. And she thought there were tears in his eyes as he went out. Ursula, I have never seen him since.

He left the house almost immediately afterwards, but no one saw him go. By some strange oversight Giles's telegram to the London bank to stop the cheque did not reach them in time. And yet Etta went herself to the telegraph office. Perhaps—as you may have heard—a tall fair young man, with a light moustache, cashed the cheque early in the afternoon. Yes, I know, Ursula, the circumstantial evidence is rather strong just here. I am quite aware that it was possible for Eric after leaving our house to be in London at the time mentioned, but no one can prove that it was Eric.

'Edgar Brown is tall and fair, and there are plenty of young men answering to that description ; and I maintain, and shall maintain to my dying day—and I am sure Mr. Cunliffe agrees with me—that it was not Eric who presented that cheque. The clerk told Giles that the young man had a scar across his cheek and a slight cut, though he was decidedly good-looking. But Giles refused to believe this. He says the clerk made a mistake about the last.

' The next morning I received a letter from

Eric, written at the Ship Hotel, Brighton, containing the exact particulars that I have given, and reiterating in the most solemn way that he was perfectly innocent of the shameful crime laid to his charge.

' " You will believe me, Gladys, I know," he went on. " You will not let my enemies blacken my memory if you can help it. If I could only be on the spot to clear up the mystery— for there is a mystery about the cheque. But I have sworn never to cross the threshold of Gladwyn again until this insult is wiped out and Giles believes in my innocence. If we never meet again, my sweet sister, you will know I loved you as well as I could love anything but I was never good and unselfish, like you. And I fear—I greatly fear—that I shall never weather through this." That was all. The letter ended abruptly.

' The following afternoon a messenger from the Ship asked to see Mr. Hamilton ; and after Giles had been closeted with him for a few minutes he came out, looking white and scared, with Eric's watch and scarf in his hands. The man had told him the young gentleman had gone out and had not returned, and they

had been found on the beach, at the extreme
end of Hove, and they feared something had
happened to him. He had ordered dinner at
a certain time, but he had not made his appearance. The next morning they had heard
reports in the town that caused them to institute
enquiries. A letter in the pocket of the coat,
directed to Eric Hamilton, Gladwyn, Heathfield,
enabled them to communicate with his relatives.
And they had lost no time in doing so. I never
saw Giles so terribly upset. He looked as
though he had received a blow. He went to
Brighton at once, and afterwards to London,
and employed every means to set our fears at
rest, for a horrible suspicion that he had really
made away with himself was in all our minds.

'I was far too ill to notice all that went on.
A fever seemed about me, and I could not eat
or sleep. I think I should have done neither,
that my poor brain must have given way under
the shock of my apprehensions, but for Mr.
Cunliffe.

'He was a true friend; a good Samaritan.
He bound up my wounds and poured in oil and
wine of divinest charity. He did not believe
that Eric was guilty, either of dishonesty or

self-destruction. In his own mind he was inclined to believe that he wished us to think him dead. It was all a mystery; but we must wait and pray; and in time he managed to instil a faint hope into my mind that this might be so.

'Etta was rather kind to me just then. She looked ill and worried, and seemed taken up with Giles. It was well that he should have some one to look after his comforts, for there was a breach between us that seemed as though it would never be healed. I saw that he was irritable and miserable; that the thought of Eric robbed him of all peace. But I could make no effort to console him, for I felt as though my heart was breaking. I'—and here she hid her face in her hands and I could see she was weeping, and I begged her earnestly to say no more, that I quite understood, and she might be sure of my sympathy with her and Eric. She kissed me gratefully, and said, 'Yes, I know. I am glad to have told you all this. Now you understand why I am so grateful to Mr. Cunliffe. Why I am so sorry'—and here her lips quivered—'if I disappoint him. I feel as though he has given me back Eric from the dead. It is true I doubt sometimes, when I am ill or gloomy, but generally my faith is strong enough to withstand Etta's incredulity.'

' Does Miss Darrell believe that he is dead ?'

' Yes; and she is so angry if any one doubts the fact. I don't know why she hates the poor boy so—even Mr. Cunliffe has reproved her for her want of charity. I think she fears Mr. Cunliffe more than any one, even Giles; she is always so careful what she says before him.'

' Gladys, I think I hear your brother's voice in the hall, and your cheeks are quite wet; he will wonder what we have been talking about.'

' I will ring for Thornton, and the tea; he shall find me clearing the table—don't offer to help me, Ursula.' And I sat still obediently, watching her slow, graceful movements about the room in the firelight; her fair hair shone like a halo of gold, and the dark ruby gown she wore gathered richer and deeper tints. That beautiful, sad face, how I should miss it !

It was some little time before Mr. Hamilton entered the room. Thornton had lighted the candles and arranged the tea-tray, and Gladys had placed herself at the table.

He testified no surprise at seeing me, but

walked to the fire, after greeting me, and warmed himself.

'They told me you were here,' he said abruptly; 'I was at the cottage just now. Have you not had your tea? Why, it is quite late, Gladys, and I want to take Miss Garston away.'

'Is there anything the matter, Mr. Hamilton?' for I was beginning to understand his manner better now.

'Oh! I have some business for you, that is all—another patient, but I will not tell you about it yet; you must have a good meal before you go out into the cold. I shall ring the bell for some more bread and butter; I know you dined early; and this hot cake will do you no good,' and as I saw he meant to be obeyed, I tried to do justice to the delicious brown bread and butter, but our conversation had taken away my appetite.

He stood over me rather like a sentinel until I had finished.

'Now then, I may as well tell you. Susan Locke is ill—acute pneumonia. I have just been down to see her, and I am afraid it is a sharp attack. Well, if you are ready, we may as well be going; the neighbour who is with her seems a poor sort of body. They sent for you, but Mrs. Barton said you were with Elspeth, and when Kitty went there, you were nowhere to be found.'

CHAPTER XXIV.

WEEPING MAY ENDURE FOR A NIGHT.

 COULD not suppress an exclamation when Mr. Hamilton mentioned the name.

Susan Locke! Poor, simple, loving-hearted Susan! What would become of Phebe if she died?

Mr. Hamilton seemed to read my thoughts.

'Yes,' he said, looking at me attentively, 'I knew you would be sorry; Miss Locke was a great favourite of yours. Poor woman, it is a sad business. I am afraid she is very ill; they ought to have sent for me before. Now, if you are ready, we will start at once.'

'I will not keep you another minute; good-bye, Ursula,' and Gladys kissed me, and

quietly followed us to the door. It was snow-
ing fast, and the ground was already white with
the fallen flakes. Mr. Hamilton put up his
umbrella, and stood waiting for me under the
shrubs, but a sudden impulse made me linger.

Gladys was still standing in the porch; her
fair hair shone like a halo in the soft lamplight,
her eyes were fixed on the falling snow. I had
said good-bye to her so hastily; I ran back,
and kissed her again.

'I wish you were not going, Gladys; I shall
miss you so.'

'It is nice to hear that,' she returned
gently; 'I shall remember those words, Ursula.
Write to me often; your letters will be my
only comfort. There, Giles is looking impatient; do not keep him waiting, dear,' and
she drew back, and a moment afterwards I
heard the door shut behind us.

Mr. Hamilton did not speak as I joined
him, and I thought that our walk would be a
silent one, until he said, presently, in rather a
peculiar tone—

'Well, Miss Garston, I suppose I ought to
congratulate you for succeeding where I have
failed.' Of course I knew what he meant, but

I pretended to misunderstand him, and he went on—

'You have won my sister's heart. Gladys cares for few people, but she seems very fond of you.'

'The feeling is reciprocated, I can assure you.'

'I am glad to know that,' he returned heartily. 'I only wish you could teach Gladys to be like other girls; she is too young and too pretty to take such grave views of life; it is unnatural at her age. One disappointment, however bitter, ought not to cloud her whole existence. Try to make her see things in a more reasonable light. Gladys is as good as gold. Of course I know that she is a fine creature, but it is not like a Christian to mourn over the inevitable in this undisciplined way.'

He spoke with great feeling, and with a gentleness that surprised me. I felt sure then of his affection for his young sister; I wished Gladys could have heard him speak in this fatherly manner. But in spite of my sympathy it was difficult for me to answer him. I felt that this was a subject that I could not discuss with Mr. Hamilton, and yet he seemed to wish me to speak.

'You must give her time to recover herself,' I said, rather lamely. 'Gladys is very sensitive; she is more delicately organised than most people; her feelings are unusually deep. She has had a severe shock; it will not be easy to comfort her.

'No, I suppose not,' with a sigh; 'her faith has suffered shipwreck; but you must try to win her back to peace—oh! you have much to do at Gladwyn as well as other places. I want you to feel at home with us, Miss Garston. Some of us have our faults, we want knowing, but you must try and like us better, and then you will not find us ungrateful.'

He stopped rather abruptly, as though he expected an answer, but I only stammered out that he was very kind, and that I hoped when Gladys returned from Bournemouth that I should often see her.

'Oh, to be sure,' he returned hastily, 'I forgot that her absence would make a differ- ence. You do not like poor Etta—I have noticed that. Well, perhaps she is a little fussy and managing; but she is a kind-hearted

creature, and very good to us all. I do not
know what I should have done without her;
my sisters do not understand me, they are never
at their ease with me. I feel this a trouble;
I want to be good to them; but there always
seems a barrier that one cannot break down.
I suppose,' with intense bitterness, ' they lay
the blame of that poor boy's death at my door,
as though I would not give my right hand to
have him back again.'

' Oh, no, Mr. Hamilton,' I exclaimed,
shocked to hear him speak in this way, ' things
are not so bad as that. I know Gladys would
be more to you if she could,' but he turned
upon me almost fiercely.

'Do not tell me that,' he said harshly,
' for I cannot believe you. Gladys cared
more for Eric's little finger than the whole of
us put together; she looks upon me as his
destroyer, as a hard taskmaster, who oppressed
him and drove him out of his home. Oh,
you want to contradict me; you would tell
me how gentle Gladys is, and how submissive.
No, she is never angry, but her looks and
words are cold, as this frozen snow; she has
not kissed me of her own accord since Eric

left us. I sometimes think that it is painful for her to live under my roof.'

'Mr. Hamilton!'

'Well, what now?' in the same repellent tone.

'You are wrong; you are unjust. Gladys does not feel like that; she has tried to forgive you in her heart for any past mistake; she sees you regret much that has passed, and she is no longer bitter against you. I wish you would believe this. I wish you could understand that she, too, longs to break down the barrier. Perhaps I ought not to say it—but I think Miss Darrell keeps you apart from your sisters.'

'What, Etta!' in an astonished tone, 'why, she is always making excuses for Gladys' coldness. Come, Miss Garston, I cannot have you misunderstand my poor little cousin in this way. You have no idea how faithful and devoted she is. She has actually refused a most advantageous offer of marriage to remain with us. She told me this in confidence; the girls do not know it—perhaps I ought not to have repeated it; but you undervalue Etta. Few women would sacrifice themselves so entirely for their belongings.'

'No, indeed,' was my reply to this; but I secretly marvelled at this piece of intelligence, and there was no time to ask any question, for we had reached the cottage, and the next minute I was standing by Susan Locke's bedside.

There was no need to tell me that poor Susan was in danger; the inflammation ran high; the flushed face, the difficult breathing, the strength and fulness of the rapid pulse, filled me with grave forebodings. Mr. Hamilton remained with me some time, and when he took his leave he promised to come again as early as possible in the morning.

'I will stay altogether if you wish it,' he said kindly, 'if you feel the least uneasiness at being alone.' But I disclaimed all fear on this score. I only begged him to remain with the patient a few minutes while I spoke to Phebe, and he agreed to this.

It was late; but I knew she would not be asleep. How could she sleep, poor soul, with this fresh stroke threatening her! As I opened the door I heard her calling to me in a voice broken with sobs.

'Oh, Miss Garston, I have been longing

for you to come to me ; you have been here for hours. I have been lying listening to your footsteps overhead ; do you know, the suspense is killing me ?'

'Yes, I am so sorry for you, Phebe ; it is hard to bear, is it not ? But I could not leave your sister. We are doing all we can to ease her sufferings, but she is very, very ill.'

'Do you think that I do not know that— she is dying, my only sister is dying,' and here her tears burst out again. 'Ah, Miss Garston, those dreadful words are coming true after all.'

'What words, my poor Phebe?' and I knelt down by her side and smoothed the hair from her damp forehead.

'Oh, you know what I mean. I have re- peated them before ; they haunt me day and night, and you refused to take them back. "If we will not lie still under His hand, and learn the lesson He would teach us, fresh trials may be sent to humble us,"—fresh trials ; and, O my God, Susan is dying !'

'You must not say that to her nurse, Phebe, you must try and strengthen my hands ; indeed, all hope is not lost, the inflammation is very high, but who knows if your prayers may not save her.'

'My prayers, my prayers,' covering her face while the tears trickled through her wasted fingers, 'as though God would listen to me who have been a rebel all my life.'

'Ah, but you are not rebellious now; you have fought against Him all these years, but now all His waves and billows have gone over your head, and you cannot breast them alone.'

'No, and I have deserved it all. I do try to pray, Miss Garston—I do, indeed, but the words will not come. I can only say over and over again, " Father, I have sinned against Heaven and before Thee," and then I stop and my heart seems breaking.'

'Well, and what can be better than that cry of your poor despairing heart to your Father! Do you think that He will not have pity on His suffering child? Be generous in your penitence, Phebe, and trust yourself and Susan in His hands.'

'Ah, but you do not know all,' she continued, fixing her miserable eyes on me. 'I have not been good to Susan—I have let her sacrifice her life for me, and have taken it all as a matter of course. I made her bear all my bad tempers and never gave her a good word. She was too tired—ah, she was often tired—and then she took this chill—and I made her wait on me all the same. She told me she was ill and in great pain, and I kept her standing for a long time—and I would not bid her good-night when she went away—and I heard her sigh as she closed the door, and I called her back and she did not hear me—and now——' but here hysterical sobs checked her utterance.

'Yes, but you are sorry now, and Susan has forgiven you. I think she wanted to send you a message, but she is in too great pain to speak. I heard her say " poor Phebe," but I begged her not to make the effort; you see she is thinking of you still.'

'My poor Susan! But she must not miss you; I am wicked and selfish to keep you like this. Go to her, Miss Garston!' And I was thankful to be dismissed.

My heart was full when I re-entered the sick-room. Mr. Hamilton looked rather scrutinising as he rose to give me his place.

'Your thoughts must be here,' he said meaningly. 'Forgive me, if I give you that hint; do not forget Providence is watching over that other room—one duty at a time, Miss Garston;' and though I coloured at this wholesome rebuke I knew he was correct.

'Yes, he is right,' I thought, as I stood listening to poor Susan's oppressed and difficult breathing; 'the Divine Teacher is beside His child; it is not for us to question this discipline or plead for an easier lesson;' but none the less did the fervent petition rise from my heart, that the angel of death might not be suffered to enter this house.

The night wore on, but, alas! there was no improvement. When Mr. Hamilton came through the snow the next morning he looked grave and dissatisfied, and then he asked me if I wanted any help, but I shook my head. 'Mrs. Martin is in the house; she will look after Phebe and Kitty.'

When he had gone, I wrote a little note and gave it to Kitty—

'I cannot leave Susan for a minute, she is so very ill. Mr. Hamilton can see no improvement, he is coming again at mid-day. She suffers very much; but we will not give up hope, you and I,' and I bade Kitty carry it to her aunt.

When Mr. Hamilton returned, he brought a little covered basket with him, and bade me rather peremptorily take my luncheon while he watched beside the patient.

This act of thoughtfulness touched me, I wondered who had packed the basket; there was the wing of a chicken, some delicate slices of tongue, a roll, and some jelly; a little note lay at the bottom—

'Giles has asked me to provide a tempting luncheon; he says you have had a sad night with poor Miss Locke, and are looking very tired. Poor Ursula—you are spending all your strength on other people.

'In another half-hour I shall leave Gladwyn. I think I am glad to go, things are so miserable here, and one loses patience sometimes. I wish I could know poor Susan Locke's fate before I go; but Giles seems to have little hope. Take care of yourself for my sake, Ursula. I have grown to love you very dearly.

'Your affectionate friend,

'GLADYS.'

Mr. Hamilton came again early in the evening, and I took the opportunity of paying Phebe another visit.

She was lying with her eyes closed, and looked very ill and exhausted—alarmingly so, I thought ; her emotion had nearly spent itself, and she was now passive and waiting for the worst.

'Let me know when it happens,' she whispered. 'I have no hope now, but I will try and bear it,' and she drew my hands to her lips and kissed them—' they have touched Susan, they are doing my work, they are blessed hands to me—' and then she seemed unable to bear more.

When Mr. Hamilton paid his final visit he announced his intention of remaining in the house. 'There will be a change one way or another before long, and I shall not leave you by yourself to-night,' he said quietly ; and in my heart I was not sorry to hear this. He told me that there was a good fire downstairs, and that he meant to take possession of a very comfortable arm-chair, but that he wanted to remain in the sick-room for half an hour or so.

I fancied that his professional eyes had

already detected some change. Presently he walked away to the fireplace and stood looking down into the flames in rather an absent way.

I could not help looking at him once or twice, he seemed so absorbed in thought; his dark face looked rigid, his lips firmly closed, and his forehead slightly puckered.

More than once I had puzzled myself over a fancied resemblance of Mr. Hamilton to some picture I had seen. All at once I remembered the subject. It was the picture of a young Christian sleeping peacefully just before he was called to his combat with wild beasts in the amphitheatre, the keeper was even then opening the door, the lions were waiting for their prey—the face was boyish—but still Mr. Hamilton reminded me of him. And there was a picture of St. Augustine sitting with his mother Monica—that reminded me of Mr. Hamilton too. I had called him plain, and Jill thought him positively ugly, but after all there was something noble in his expression, a power that made itself felt.

Just then the lines of his face relaxed and softened; he half smiled, looked up, and our eyes met. I was terribly abashed at the thought that he should find me watching him; but to my surprise his face brightened, and he roused himself and crossed the room.

'I was dreaming, I think, but you woke me. Are you very tired, shall I take your place?' but before I could reply his manner changed and he stooped over the bed, and then looked at me with a smile.

'I thought so. The breathing is certainly less difficult, the inflammation is diminishing. I see signs of improvement.'

'Thank God!' was my answer to this, and before long this hope was verified; the pain and difficulty of breathing was certainly less intense, the danger was subsiding.

Mr. Hamilton went downstairs soon after this, and I settled to my solitary night-watch, but it was no longer dreary—every hour I felt more assured that Susan Locke would be restored to her sister.

Once or twice during the night I crept into Phebe's room to gladden her heart with the glad news, but she was sleeping heavily and I would not disturb her. 'Weeping may endure for a night, but joy cometh in the morning,' I said to myself, as I sat down by Susan's bedside.

I was very weary, but a strange tumult of thoughts seemed surging through my brain, and I was unable to control them. Gladys' pale face and tear-filled eyes rose perpetually before me—her low passionate tones vibrated in my ear. 'They have accused him falsely,' I seemed to hear her say ; 'Eric never took that cheque.'

What a mystery in that quiet household ; no wonder there was something unrestful in the atmosphere of Gladwyn—that one felt oppressed and ill at ease in that house.

Fragments of my conversation with Mr. Hamilton came unbidden to my memory. How strange that that proud, reserved man should have spoken so to me, that he had suffered his heart's bitterness to overflow in words to me, who was almost a stranger :—' They lay the blame of that poor boy's death at my door, as though I would not give my right hand to have him back again.' Oh ! if Gladys had only heard the tone in which he said this, she must have believed and have been sorry for him.

' They are too hard upon him,' I said to myself. 'If he has been stern and injudicious with his poor young brother, he has long ago repented of his hardness. He is very good to them all, but they will not try to understand him; it is not right of Gladys to treat him as a stranger. I am sorry for them all, but I begin to feel that Mr. Hamilton is not the only one to blame.'

I wished I could have told him this, but I knew the words would never get themselves spoken. I might be sorry for him in my heart, but I could never tell him so, never assure him of my true sympathy. I was far too much in awe of him—there are some men one would never venture to pity.

But all the same I longed to do him some secret service; he had been kind to me, and had helped me much in my work. If I could only succeed in bringing him and Gladys nearer together, if I could make them understand each other, I felt I would have spared no pains or trouble to do so.

If he were not so infatuated on the subject of his cousin's merits, I thought scornfully, I should be more sanguine about my success, but Miss Darrell had hoodwinked him completely. As long as he believed in all she chose to tell him, Gladys would never be in her proper place.

As soon as it was light I heard Mr. Hamilton

stirring in the room below; he came up for a moment to tell me that he was going home to breakfast; he looked quite fresh and brisk, and declared he had had a capital night's sleep.

'I am going to find some one to take your place while you go home and have a good seven hours' rest,' he said in his decided way. 'I suppose you are aware that you have not slept for forty-eight hours. Kitty is going to make you some tea,' and with this he took himself off.

I went into Phebe's room presently. Kitty told me that she was awake at last. As soon as she saw me she put up her hands as though to ward off my approach.

'Wait a moment,' she said huskily, 'you need not tell me, I know what you have come to say—I have no longer a sister—Susan is a saint in heaven.'

For a moment I hesitated, afraid to speak. She had nerved herself to bear the worst, and I feared the revulsion of feeling would be too great. As I stood there silently looking down at her drawn haggard face, I felt she would not have had strength to bear a fresh trial. If Susan had died Phebe would not have long survived her.

'You are wrong,' I said very gently, 'I have no bad news for you this morning; the inflammation has diminished. Susan breathes more easily, each breath is no longer acute agony.'

'Do you mean that she is better?' staring at me incredulously.

'Most certainly she is better, the danger is over; but we must be very careful, for she will be ill for some time yet. Yes, indeed, Phebe, you may believe me—do you think I would deceive you? God has heard your prayers, and Susan is spared to you.'

I never saw a human countenance so transformed as Phebe's was that moment; every feature seemed to quiver with ecstasy, she could not speak, only she folded her hands as though in prayer. Presently she looked up, and said as simply as a child:

'Oh, I am so happy! I never thought I should be happy again. You may leave me now, Miss Garston, for I want to thank God for the first time in my life. I feel as though I must love Him now for giving Susan back to me,' and then again she begged me to leave her.

Mr. Hamilton did not forget me. I had just put the sick-room in order when a respectable young woman made her appearance. She told me that her name was Carron, that she was a married woman and a friend of Miss Locke's, and she would willingly take my place until evening.

I was thankful to accept this timely offer of help, and went home, and enjoyed a deep dreamless sleep for some hours. When I woke it was evening. Jill was standing by my bedside with a tray in her hands, the room was bright with firelight; Jill's big eyes looked at me affectionately.

'How you have slept, Ursie dear ; just like a baby! I have been in and out half a dozen times; but no, you never stirred. I told Mr. Hamilton so, when he inquired an hour ago. Now you are to drink this coffee, and when you are quite awake I will give you his message.'

'I am quite awake now,' I returned, rubbing my eyes vigorously.

'Well then, let me see. Oh, Miss Locke is going on well, and Mrs. Carron will stop with her until eight o'clock. Phebe has been ill, and they sent for him; but it was only faintness and palpitation, and she is better now. He has been to see Elspeth, and she is poorly; but there is no need for you to trouble about her. Miss Darrell is sending her broth and jelly, and Peggy waits on her very nicely. Lady Betty and I went to see her to-day, and she was as comfortable and cheery as possible, and told us that she felt like a lady in that big bed downstairs. Mr. Hamilton says she will not die just yet, but one of these days she will go off as quietly as a baby. She asked after you, Ursie, and sent you a power of love, and I hope it will do you good.'

'And what have you been doing with yourself all day, Jill?' I asked rather anxiously.

'Oh, lots of things,' tossing back her thick locks. 'Let me see —Lady Betty came to fetch me for a walk, and we met Mr. Tudor. He is all alone, poor man, and very dull without Mr. Cunliffe; he told us so, so Lady Betty brought him back to lunch. And Miss Darrell was so cross, and told poor Lady Betty that she was very forward to do such a thing—they had such a quarrel in the drawing-room about it. Mr. Tudor came in and found Lady Betty crying, so he made us come out in the garden, and we played a new sort of Aunt Sally. Mr.

Tudor stuck up an old hat of Mr. Hamilton's
—at least we found out it was not an old
one after all—and we snowballed it, and Mr.
Hamilton came out and helped us.   After tea,
we all told ghost stories round the fire.   Miss
Darrell does not like them, so she went up to
her room.   Mr. Tudor had to see a sick man,
but he came back to dinner; but I would
not stay, for I thought you would be waking,
Ursie, so Mr. Hamilton brought me home.'

'Jill!' I asked desperately, 'have they
not written for you to join them at Hastings
yet? I begin to think you have been idle long
enough.'

'Had you not better go to sleep again,
Ursie, dear?' returned Jill, marching off with my
tray.   But she made a little face at me as she
went out of the door.   'I shall get into trouble
over this,' I thought.   'I really must write
to Aunt Philippa;' but I was spared the neces-
sity, for the very next day Jill came to me at
Miss Locke's to tell me, with a very long face,
that her mother had written to say that Miss
Gillespie was coming the following week, and
Jill was to pack up and join them at Hastings
the very next day.

CHAPTER XXV.

'THERE IS NO ONE LIKE DONALD.'

MRS. CARRON very kindly took my place that I might be with Jill that last evening, and we spent it in Jill's favourite fashion, talking in the firelight.

She was a little quiet and subdued, full of regret at leaving me, and more affectionate than ever.

'I have never been so happy in my life,' she said in rather a melancholy voice; 'when I get to Hastings, my visit here will seem like a dream, it has been so nice somehow; you are such a dear old thing, Ursula, and I am so fond of Lady Betty. I shall ask mother to invite her in the holidays.'

'And there is no one else you will regret,

Jill?' I asked, anxious to sound her on one point.

'Oh, yes; I am sorry to bid good-bye to Mr. Tudor, he has been such fun lately, I really do think he is quite the nicest young man I know.'

'Do you know many young men, my dear?' was my apparently innocent remark; but Jill was not deceived by this smooth speech.

'Of course I do,' in a scornful voice; ' they come to see Sara, and I hate them so, flimsy stuck-up creatures, with their white ties and absurd little moustaches—each one is more stupid and vapid than the other—and Sara must think so too, for she smiles on them all alike.'

'You are terribly hard on the young men of your generation, Jill; I daresay I should think them very harmless and pleasant;' but she shook her head vigorously.

' Why cannot they be natural, and say good-natured things like Mr. Tudor—he is real, and not make-believe, pretending that he is too bored to live at all—one would think there was no truth anywhere, nothing but tinsel and

sham to listen to them; that is why I like
Mr. Tudor, he has the ring of the true metal
about him—even Miss Darrell agrees with me
there.'

'Do you discuss Mr. Tudor with Miss
Darrell?'

'Why not?' opening her eyes widely. ' I
like to talk about my friends, and I feel
Mr. Tudor is a real friend. She was so interested—really interested, I mean, without any
humbug—at least pretence,' for here I held up
my finger at Jill; 'she wanted to know if you
liked him too, and I said, " Oh, yes, so much,
he was a great favourite of yours," and she
seemed pleased to hear it.'

'You silly child, I wish you would leave
me and my likes and dislikes out of your
conversations with Miss Darrell.'

'Well, do you know, I try to do so, because
I know how you hate her—at least dislike her,
that is a more ladylike term—you are so
horribly particular, Ursula; but somehow your
name always gets in, and I never know how,
and there is no keeping you out. Sometimes
she makes me dreadfully angry about you, and
sometimes she says nice things; but there, we

will not talk about the double-faced lady to
night—J understand her less than ever.'

We glided into more serious subjects after
this. I made Jill promise to be more patient
with her life, and work from a greater sense
of duty, and I begged her most earnestly to
fight against discontent, and exorcise this
youthful demon of hers, and again she promised to do her best.

'I feel better about things somehow; you
have done me good, Ursie, you always do. I
must make mother understand that I am
nearly a woman, and that I do not intend to
waste my time any longer dreaming childish
dreams. I suppose mother is really fond of
me, though she does find fault with me continually, and is always praising Sara.' Jill
went on talking in this way for some time,
and then we went upstairs together.

I was rather provoked to find Mr. Tudor
at the station the next morning. I suppose my
steady look abashed him, for he muttered something about Smith's bookstall, as though I
should be deceived by such a flimsy excuse.
After all, Mr. Tudor was not better than other
young men; in spite of Jill's praises, he was

capable of this mild subterfuge to get his own way.

Jill was so honestly and childishly pleased to see him, that I ought to have been disarmed. She went off with him to the bookstall, while I looked after her luggage, and they stood there chattering and laughing until I joined them, and then Mr. Tudor grew suddenly quiet.

As the train came up, I heard him ask Jill how long they were to stay at Hastings, and if they would be at Hyde Park Gate before Easter.

' I shall be up in town then,' he remarked carelessly, ' to see some of my people.'

' Oh yes, and you must come and see us,' she returned cheerfully. ' Good-bye, Mr. Tudor. I am so sorry to leave Heathfield.'

But after all Jill's last look was for me—as she leant out of the carriage waving her hand, she did not even glance at the young man, who was standing silent and gloomy beside me. I felt rather sorry for the poor boy, as he turned away quite sadly.

' I must go down to the schools ; good-bye, Miss Garston,' he said hurriedly—one would have thought he had to make up for lost

time, as he strode through the station and up
the long road. Had Jill really taken his
fancy, I wondered—had her big eyes and quaint
speeches bewitched him? Mr. Tudor was a
gentleman, and we all liked him; but what
would Uncle Brian and Aunt Philippa say if
a needy, good-looking young curate were
suddenly to present himself as a lover for their
daughter Jocelyn; why Jill would be rich
some day—poor Ralph was dead, and she and
Sara would be co-heiresses—her parents would
expect her to make a grand match.

I shook my head gravely over poor
Lawrence's prospects as I took my way slowly
up the hill. I was rather glad when his broad
shoulders were out of sight; I should be sorry
if any disappointment were to cloud his cheery
nature.

I missed Jill a great deal at first, but in my
heart I was not sorry to get rid of the responsibility; a lively girl of sixteen, with strong
individuality and marked precocity, is likely
to be a formidable charge; but Mrs. Barton
lamented her absence in no measured terms.

'It seems so dull without Miss Jocelyn,' she
said, the first evening. 'She was such a lively

young lady, and made us all cheerful. Why, she would run in and out the kitchen a dozen times a day, to feed the chickens, or pet the cat, or watch me knead the bread. She and Nathaniel got on famously together, and often and often I have found her helping him with the books, and laughing so merrily when he made a mistake. I used to think Nathaniel did it on purpose sometimes, just for the fun of it.'

Yes, we all missed Jill, and I for one loved the girl dearly. It made me quite happy one day when she wrote a long letter, telling me that she was delighted with her new governess.

'Miss Gillespie is as nice as possible,' she wrote. 'I already feel quite fond of her; my lessons are as interesting now as they used to be dull with Fräulein. She knows a great deal, and is not ashamed to confess when she is ignorant of anything; she says right out that she cannot answer my questions, and proposes that we should study it together. I quite enjoy our walks and talks, for she takes so much interest in all I tell her. She is a little dull and sad sometimes, as though she were thinking of past troubles, but I like to feel that I can cheer her up and do her good. Mother and Sara are delighted with her; she plays so beautifully, and they say that she is such a gentlewoman. When we come downstairs in the evening she will not allow me to creep into a corner—she makes me join in the conversation, and coaxes me to play my pieces ; and she tries to prevent mother making horrid little remarks on my awkwardness.

' " It will all come right, Mrs. Garston," I heard her say one day. " It is far wiser not to notice it; young girls are so sensitive, and Jocelyn is keenly alive to her shortcomings." And mother actually nodded assent to this, and the next moment she called me up, and said how much I had improved in my playing, and that Colonel Ferguson had told her that I had been exceedingly well taught.

' By the bye, I am quite sure that Colonel Ferguson intends to be my brother-in-law ; he is always here in the evening, and yesterday he sent Sara such a magnificent bouquet.'

Jill's chatty letters were always amusing. She had prepared me beforehand, so I was not surprised at receiving a voluminous letter from Aunt Philippa a few days afterwards, informing me of Sara's engagement to Colonel Ferguson.

'Your uncle and I are delighted with the match,' she wrote. 'Colonel Ferguson belongs to a very good old family, and he has private property. Your uncle says that he is a very intelligent man, and is much respected in the regiment.

'Mrs. Fullerton thinks it is a pity for Sara to marry a widower; but I call that nonsense; he is a young-looking man for his age, and every one thinks him so handsome. Sara, poor darling, is as happy as possible. I believe that they are to be married soon after Easter, as he wants to get some salmon-fishing in Norway; so we shall come up to Hyde Park Gate early next week, and see about the trousseau, for there is no time to be lost.'

Sara added a few words in her pretty girlish handwriting.

'I wonder if you will be very much surprised by mamma's letter, Ursula dear. We all thought he liked Lesbia, but no, he says that was entirely a mistake on our part, he never really thought of her at all.

'Of course I am very happy. I think there is no one like Donald in the world. I cannot imagine why such a wise, clever man should

fall in love with a silly little body like me. I
suppose I must please him in some way, for,
really, he seems dreadfully in love.

'You must come to my wedding, Ursula,
and I must choose your dress for you; of
course, father will pay for it, but I promise you
it shall be pretty, and suitable to your com-
plexion. I mean to have eight bridesmaids.
Jocelyn will be one, of course, and I shall get
that tall, fair Grace Underley to act as a foil to
her bigness. I shall not ask poor Lesbia to
be one—it would be too trying for her, and I
know you will not care about it ; but you must
come for a week, and see all my pretty things,
and help poor mamma, for she has only
Jocelyn—so remember you are to keep yourself disengaged the week after Easter.'

I wrote back that same evening warm con-
gratulations to Sara and Aunt Philippa, and
promised to come when Sara wanted me. A
gay wedding was not to my taste, but I knew I
owed this duty to them—they had been kind to
me in their own fashion, and according to their
lights, and I would not fail them. Easter would
fall late this year—in the middle of April—
there were still three months before Sara would

be married, and most likely by that time I should need a few days rest and change.

The next morning I heard from Lesbia. It was a kind, sad little letter; she told me she was glad about Sara's engagement, and as they were still at Hastings she and her mother had called at Warrior Square, and had found Sara and her *fiancé* together.

'I think it has improved Sara already,' it went on; 'she was looking exceedingly pretty, and in good spirits, and she seemed very proud of her tall, grave-looking soldier. Mother and I always liked Colonel Ferguson. He and Sara are complete contrasts; I think her brightness and good humour, as well as her beauty, have attracted him, for he is honestly in love ! I liked the quiet, deferential way in which he treated her. I am sure he will make a kind husband. Mrs. Garston looked as happy as possible. I did not see Jocelyn; she was out riding with her father.

'We are going down to dear Rutherford in March, but I have promised Sara to come up for the wedding. Don't sigh, Ursula—it is all in the day's work, and one has to do trying things sometimes.

'I have come to think that perhaps dear
Charlie is better off where he is. He was so
enthusiastic and so true that life must have
disappointed him. Perhaps I should have
disappointed him too—but, no, I should have
loved him too well to do that.

'I shall love to be at Rutherford during the
spring. Everything will remind me of those
sweet spring days two years ago. Oh, those
walks and rides, and the evening when we
listened to the nightingale, and he told me that
he loved me. I remember the very patch of
grass where I stood. There was a little clump
of alders, and I can see how he looked then.
Oh, Ursula, these memories are very sad, but
they are sweet, too—for Charlie is our Charlie
still, is he not?'

'Poor Lesbia!' I sighed, as I folded up her
letter and prepared for my day's work. It
must be hard for her to witness Sara's happiness, when her own life is so clouded. Her
heart is still true to Charlie; but she is so
young, and life is so long. I trust that better
things are in store for her.'

Miss Locke was recovering very slowly.
Years of anxiety and hard work had over-taxed

her strength sorely. Mr. Hamilton used to shake his head over her tardy progress, and tell her that she was a very unsatisfactory patient, and that he had expected to cure her long before this.

'If it were not for you and my dear Miss Garston, I should never be lying here now,' she returned gratefully. 'I must have died—you know that, Doctor—and even now, in spite of all the good things you send me, I am so weary and fit for nothing I feel as though I should never sit up again.'

'Oh, we shall have you up before long,' he returned cheerfully. 'You are only rather slow about it. You are not troubling about your work or anything else, I hope, because the rent is paid, and there is plenty in the cupboard for Phebe and Kitty.'

'I know you have paid the rent, and I shall never be grateful enough to you, Doctor; for what should I have done, with this long illness making me behindhand with everything? I am afraid Miss Garston puts her hand in her pocket sometimes. I hope the Lord will bless you both for your goodness to two helpless women. Ay! and He will bless you, Doctor!'

'I am sure I hope so,' he returned in a good-humoured tone, shaking her hand. ' There! mind what your nurse says and keep yourself easy ; you will find Phebe a different person when you see her next.'

I was afraid Phebe would find her sister much changed when they met. Miss Locke had greatly aged since her illness ; her hair was much greyer, and her face was sunken, and I doubted whether she would ever be the same woman again. Mr. Hamilton and I had already discussed the sisters' future.

' I am afraid they will be terribly pinched,' he said once. ' Miss Locke is suffering now from years of overwork. She will never be able to work as hard as she has done. And she has to provide for that child, Kitty, as well as for poor Phebe.'

' We must think what is to be done,' I replied. ' Miss Locke is a very good manager ; she is careful and thrifty. A little will go a long way with her.'

Mr. Hamilton said no more on the subject just then, but a few days afterwards he told me that he intended to buy the cottage. He had a good deal of house property in Heathfield, and a cottage more or less did not matter to him.

'They shall live in it rent free, and I will take care of the repairs. There will be no need for Miss Locke to work so hard then. She is a good woman, and I thoroughly respect her. Of course, I know she is a favourite of yours, Miss Garston, but you must not think that influences me.'

'As though I should imagine such a thing!' I returned, in quite an affronted tone. But Mr. Hamilton only laughed.

'You are such an insignificant person, you see,' he went on mischievously. 'You are of so little use to your generation. People do not benefit by your example, or defer to your opinion. There is no St. Ursula in the calendar.' Now what did he mean by all this rigmarole? But he only laughed again in a provoking way and went out.

I had had both the sisters on my hands. Those hours of fearful suspense had told on Phebe, and for a week or two we were very anxious about her.

I kept the extent of her illness from Susan, and she never knew that Mr. Hamilton visited her daily. Strange to say, Phebe gave us little trouble. She bore her bodily sufferings with surprising patience, and even made light of them; and she would thank me most gratefully when I waited on her.

I was never long in her room. There was no reading or singing now. Nothing would induce her to keep me from Susan. She used to beg me to go back to Susan and leave her to Kitty. I never forgot Susan's look of astonishment when I told her this.

'Somehow, it doesn't sound like Phebe,' she said, looking at me a little wistfully. 'Are you sure you understand her, Miss Garston—that something has not put her out? She has often sulked with me like that.'

'Oh! Phebe never sulks now,' I returned, smiling at this view of the case. 'She is not like the same woman, Susan. She thinks of other people now.' Miss Locke heard me silently, but I saw that she was still incredulous. She was not sanguine enough to hope for a miracle—and surely only a miracle could change Phebe's sullen and morbid nature.

The sisters were longing to meet, but the helplessness of the one and the long protracted weakness of the other kept them long apart, though only a short flight of stairs divided them.

At last I thought we might venture to bring Susan into Phebe's room.

The weather was less severe, and Susan seemed a little stronger, so Kitty and I hurried ourselves in preparation for a festive tea in Phebe's room.

She watched us with unconcealed interest as we spread the tea-cloth, and arranged the best china, and then placed an easy-chair by her bedside.

The room really looked very bright and cosy; a little grey kitten that I had brought Kitty was asleep on the quilt—Phebe had taken a great fancy to the pretty, playful little creature, and it was always with her; Kitty's large wax doll was lying with its curly head on her pillow.

Susan trembled very much as she entered the room, leaning heavily on my arm. Phebe lay quite motionless watching her as she walked slowly towards the bed, then her face suddenly grew pitiful and she held out her arms.

'Oh! how ill you look, my poor Susan, and

so old and grey; but what does it matter so that I have got my Susan back! If you had died, I should have died too; God never meant to punish me like that,' and she stroked and kissed her face as though she were a child, and for a little while the two sisters mingled their tears together.

Susan was too weak for much emotion, so I placed her comfortably in her easy-chair, and bade her look at Phebe without troubling to talk; but her heart was too full for silence.

'Why, my woman,' she burst out, 'you look real bonnie. I do believe your face has got a bit of colour in it, and you remind me of the old Phebe; nay,' as Phebe laughed at this, 'I never thought to hear you laugh again, my dearie.'

'It is with the pleasure of seeing you,' returned Phebe, 'if you only knew what I suffered while you lay ill; "there is no improvement," they said, and Miss Garston looked at me so pityingly; and if you had died and never spoke to me again—and I had refused to bid you good-night—you remember, Susan—oh! I think my heart would have broken if you had gone away and left me like that.'

'Nay, I should have thought nothing about it. but that it was just Phebe's way; do you mean that you fretted about that, lass? Oh!' turning to me, for Phebe was crying bitterly over the recollection, 'I would not believe you, Miss Garston, when you said Phebe was changed, for I said to myself, "Surely she will be up to her old tricks again soon"; but now I see you are right—nay. never fret, my bonnie woman, for I loved you when you were as tiresome and crossgrained as possible. I think I cannot help loving you,' finished Susan simply as she took her sister's hand.

That was a happy evening that we spent in Phebe's room. When tea was over we read a few chapters, Kitty and I. and then I sang some of Phebe's favourite songs. When I had finished, I looked at them : Phebe had fallen asleep with Susan's hand still in her's—there was a look of peaceful rest on the worn grey face that made me whisper to Miss Locke,

'The evil spirit is cast out at last, Susan.'

'Ay,' returned Susan quietly. 'She is

clothed and in her right mind, and I doubt not sitting at the feet of Him who has called her. I have got my Phebe back again, thank God, as I have not seen her for many a long year.'

CHAPTER XXVI.

I HEAR ABOUT CAPTAIN HAMILTON.

IT was now more than five weeks since Gladys had left us, but during that time I had heard from her frequently. Her letters were deeply interesting, she wrote freely, pouring out her thoughts on every subject without reserve. Somehow I felt, as I read them, that those letters gave as much pleasure to the writer as to the recipient, and I found afterwards that this was the case. Her consciousness of my sympathy with her made her open her heart more freely to me than to any other person. She delighted in telling me of the books she read, in describing the various effects of nature. Her descriptions were so powerful and graphic, that they quite surprised me. She made me feel as though I were walking through the fir woods beside her, or standing on the sea-shore watching the white-crested waves rolling in and breaking into foam at our feet—a sort of dewy freshness seemed to stamp the pages.   Gladys loved nature with all her heart; she revelled in the solemn grandeur of those woods, in the breadth and freedom of the ocean ; it seemed to harmonise with her varying moods.

'I feel a different creature already,' she wrote when she had been away a fortnight. ' Without owning myself happy (but happiness active or negative will never come to me again), still I am calmer and more at peace —away from the oppressive influences that surrounded me at home.'

'I have made up my mind that the atmosphere of Gladwyn is fatal to my soul's health. I seem to wither up like some sensitive plant in that blighting air ; half truths, misunderstandings, and jealousies have corroded our home peace.   I am better away from it all, for here I can own myself ill and miserable, and no one blames or misapprehends my meaning—there are no harsh judgments under the guise of pity.

'These dear people are so truly charitable, they think no evil of a poor girl who is faithful to a brother's memory—they are patient with my sad moods, they leave me free to follow out my wishes. I wander about as I will, I sketch or read, I sit idle; no one blames me; they are as good to me as you would be in their place.

'I shall stay away as long as possible, until I feel strong enough to take up my life again. You will not be vexed with me, my dear Ursula—you know how I have suffered, you of all others will sympathise with me. Think of the relief it is to wake up in the morning and feel that no jarring influences will be at work that day; that no eyes will pry into my secret sorrow, or seek to penetrate my very thoughts; that I may look and speak as I like, that my words will not be twisted to serve other people's purposes. Forgive me if I speak harshly, but indeed you do not know all yet. Your last letter made me a little sad, you speak so much of Giles. Do you really think I am hard upon him? The idea is painful to me.

'I like you to think well of him, he is a good

man. I have always thoroughly respected him, but there is no sympathy between us. Of course it is more Etta's fault than his—she has usurped my place, and Giles no longer needs me. Perhaps I am not kind to him, not sisterly or soft in my manners; but he treats me too much as a child. He never asks my opinion on any subject; we live under his protection, and he never grudges us money. He is generous in that way, but he never enters into our thoughts. Lady Betty and I lead our own lives.

'You ask me why I do not write to him, my dear Ursula. Such a thought would never enter my head. Write to Giles! what should I say to him? How would such a letter ever get itself written? Do you suppose he would care for me as a correspondent? I should like you to ask him that question, if you dared. Giles's face would be a study. I fancy I write that letter—a marvellous composition of commonplace nothings. "My dear brother, I think you will like to hear our Bournemouth news, etc." I can imagine him tossing it aside as he opens his other letters: "Gladys has actually written to me. I suppose

she wants another cheque—see what she says,
Etta. You may read it aloud if you like while
I finish my breakfast." Now, do not look
incredulous. I once saw Lady Betty's letter
treated in this way, and all her poor little
sentences pulled to pieces in Etta's usual
fashion. No, thank you, I will not write to
Giles. I write to Lady Betty sometimes, but
not often—that is why she comes to you for
news. We are a queer household, Ursula. I
am very fond of my dear little Lady Betty, but
somehow I have never enjoyed writing to her,
since Etta one day handed to her one of my
letters opened by mistake. Lady Betty has
fancied the mistake has occurred more than
once.'

I put down this letter with a sigh; it was
the only painful one I had received from
Gladys. My remark about her writing to her
brother had evidently upset her, but after this
she did not speak much about Gladwyn, and
by tacit consent we spoke little about any of
her people except Lady Betty. When I mentioned Mr. Hamilton I did so casually, and
only with reference to my own work; he was
so mixed up with my daily life. I came so

continually into contact with him that it was impossible to avoid his name.

Gladys understood this, for she once replied:

'I am really and honestly glad that you and Giles work so well together. He will be a good friend to you, I know, for when he forms a favourable opinion of a person he is slow to change it, and Giles is one who, with all his faults, will go through fire and water for his friends. I like to hear of him in this way, for you always put him in the best light, and though you may not believe it, after all my hard speeches, I am sufficiently proud of my brother to wish him to be properly appreciated,' and after this I mentioned him less reluctantly.

Max came back about ten days after Jill had left us. I found him waiting for me one evening when I got back to the cottage. As usual, he greeted me most affectionately, only he laughed when I made him turn to the light that I might see how he looked.

'Well, what is your opinion, Ursula, my dear? I hope you have noticed the grey hairs in my beard, I saw them there this morning.'

' You are rather tanned by the cold winds. I suppose Torquay has done you good; but your eyes have not lost their tired look, Max; you are not a bit rested.'

' I believe I want more work; too much rest would kill me with ennui,' stretching out his arms with a sort of weary gesture. ' I walked a great deal at Torquay; I was out in the air all day; but it did not seem to be what I wanted—I was terribly bored. Tudor is glad to get me back—the fellow actually seems dull. Have you any idea what has gone wrong with him, Ursula?' But I prudently turned a deaf ear to this question, and he did not follow it up; and a moment afterwards he mentioned that he had been at Gladwyn, and that Miss Darrell had given him a good account of Miss Hamilton.

' I had no idea that she was away until this afternoon. Her departure was rather sudden, was it not?'

I think he was glad when I gave him Gladys' message; but he looked rather grave when I told him how much she was enjoying her freedom.

' She seems a different creature; those

Maberleys are so good to her, they pet her, and yet leave her uncontrolled to follow her own wishes. I am more at rest about her there.'

'A girl ought to be happy in her own home,' he returned somewhat moodily; 'I think Miss Hamilton has indulged her sadness long enough. Perhaps there are other reasons for her being better—I suppose she has not heard——?' and here he stopped rather awkwardly.

'Do you mean whether she has heard anything of Eric? Oh no, Max.'

'No, I was not meaning that,' looking at me rather astonished. 'Of course we know the poor boy is dead. I was only wondering if she had had an Indian letter lately? Well, it is none of my affair, and I cannot wait to hear more now. Good-night, little she-bear; I am off.' And he actually was off, in spite of my calling him quite loudly in the porch, for I wanted him to tell me what he meant. Had Gladys any special correspondent in India? I wondered if I might venture to question Lady Betty.

As it very often happens, she played quite

innocently into my hands, for the very next day she came to tell me that she had had a letter from Gladys.

'It was a very short one,' she grumbled. 'Only she had an Indian letter to answer, and that took up her time, so that was a pretty good excuse for once.'

'Has Gladys any special friend in India?'

'Only Claude!—I mean our cousin, Claude Hamilton. Have you not often heard us talk of him?—how strange! Why he used to stay with us for months at a time, and he and Gladys were great friends—they correspond. He is Captain Hamilton now; his regiment was ordered to India just at the time poor dear Eric disappeared; he was awfully shocked about that, I remember. Etta wrote and told him all about it; he was a great favourite of hers. We none of us thought him handsome except Etta; he was a nice-looking fellow, but nothing else.'

'And you and Gladys are fond of him?'

'Oh yes,' but here Lady Betty looked a little queer.

'Gladys writes to him most; she has always been his correspondent. Now and then I get

a letter written to me.   You see he has no one
else belonging to him now his mother is
dead.   Aunt Agnes died about two years ago,
and he never had brothers or sisters, so he
adopted us.'

'Uncle Max knew him, of course?'

'To be sure.   Mr. Cunliffe knew all our
people—Claude was a favourite of his, too.   I
think every one liked him; he was so straight-
forward, and never did anything mean.   I
think he will make a splendid officer; he has
had fever lately, and we rather expect he is
coming home on sick leave.   Etta hopes so.'

'Gladys has never spoken of her cousin to
me.'

'That is because you two are always talking
about other things—poor Eric, for example.
Gladys likes to talk about Claude, of course—
he is her own cousin,' and Lady Betty's manner
was just a little defiant, as though I had accused Gladys of some indiscretion.   I heard
her mutter, 'They find plenty of fault with
her about that,' but I took no notice.   I had
satisfied my curiosity, and I knew now why
Max fancied an Indian letter would raise
Gladys' spirits; but all the same he might

have spoken out. Max had no business to be so mysterious with me !

I heard Captain Hamilton's name again shortly afterwards. I was calling at Gladwyn one afternoon. I was loth to do so in Gladys' absence ; but I dare not discontinue my visits entirely, for fear of Miss Darrell's remarks. To my surprise, I found her *tête-à-tête* with Uncle Max. She welcomed me with a great show of cordiality ; but before I had been five minutes in the room, I found out that my visit was inopportune, though Max seemed unfeignedly pleased to see me, and she had repeated his words in almost parrot-like fashion. ' Oh yes, I am so glad to see you, Miss Garston—it is so good of you to call when dear Gladys is away. Of course, I know she is the attraction—we all know that, do we not ? ' smiling sweetly upon me. ' She has been away more than five weeks now—dear, dear, how time flies—really five weeks, and this is your first call.'

' You know how Miss Locke's illness has engrossed me,' I remonstrated. ' I never pretend to mere conventional calls.'

' No, indeed. You have a code of your own, have you not ? Your niece is fortunate,

Mr. Cunliffe. She makes her own laws, while we poor inferior mortals are obliged to conform to the world's dictates. I wish I were strong-minded like you. It must be such a pleasure to be free, and despise *les convenances*. People are so artificial, are they not ? '

' Ursula is not artificial, at any rate,' returned Max, with a benevolent glance. It had struck me as I entered the room that he looked rather bored and ill at ease, but Miss Darrell was in high spirits, and looked almost handsome. I never saw her better dressed.

' No, indeed. Miss Garston is almost too frank—not that that is a fault. Oh yes, Miss Locke's illness has been a tedious affair ; even Giles got weary of it, and used to grumble at having to go every day. Of course, seeing Giles once or twice a day, you heard all our news, so we did not expect you to toil up here; that would have been unnecessary trouble after your hard work.'

Miss Darrell spoke quite civilly, and I do not know why her speech rankled and made me reply rather quickly,

' Nurses do not gossip with the doctor, Miss Darrell. Mr. Hamilton has told me no news, more.'

I was angry with myself when I said this, for why need I have answered her at all or taken notice of her remark; and, above all, why need I have mentioned Gladys' name? Miss Darrell's colour rose in a moment.

'Dear me! I am glad to hear dear Gladys writes to you. She does not honour us. Lady Betty gets a note sometimes, but Giles and I are never favoured with a word. Giles feels terribly hurt about it sometimes, but I tell him it is only Gladys' way. Girls are careless sometimes. Of course she does not mean to slight him.'

'Of course not,' rather gravely from Max.

'All the same, it is very neglectful on Gladys' part. If you are a real friend, Miss Garston, you will tell her what a mistake it is— really a fatal mistake, though I do not dare to tell her so. I see Giles's look of disappointment when the post brings him nothing but dry business letters. He is so anxious about her health. He let her go so willingly, and yet not one word of recognition for her own, I may say her only, brother.'

Max was looking so exceedingly grave by

this time that I longed to change the subject. I would say a word in defence of Gladys when we were alone—he and I. It would be worse than useless to speak before Miss Darrell. She would twist my words before my face. I never said a word in Gladys' behalf that she did not make me repent it.

The next moment, however, she had started on a different tack.

'Oh ! do you know, Mr. Cunliffe,' she said carelessly as she crossed the hearth-rug to ring the bell, ' we have heard again from Captain Hamilton ? '

Max raised his head quickly. 'Indeed, I hope he is quite well. By the bye, I remember you told me he had a touch of fever ; but I trust he has got the better of that.'

'We hope so,' in a very impressive tone ; ' but it was a sharp attack, and no doubt home-sickness and worry of mind accelerated the mischief. Poor Claude ! I fear he has suffered much ; not that he says so himself—he is far too proud to complain. But he is likely to come home on sick leave ; next mail will settle the question, but I believe we may expect him about the end of July.'

' Indeed, that is good news for all of you ; ' but the poker that Max had taken up fell with a little crash among the fire-irons. Miss Darrell gave a faint scream, and then laughed at her foolish nervousness.

' It was very clumsy on my part,' stammered Max. Could it be my fancy, or had he turned suddenly pale, as though something had startled him too ?

' Oh no, it was only my poor nerves,' replied Miss Darrell, with her brightest smile. ' What was I saying ? Oh yes, I remember now—about Claude—he wrote to Gladys to ask if he might come, and she said yes. Ah, here comes tea, and I believe I heard Giles's ring at the bell.'

I cannot tell which of the two revealed it to me—whether it was the sudden pallor on Max's face, or the curious watchful look that I detected in Miss Darrell's eyes—it was only there for a moment, but it reminded me of the look with which a cat eyes the mouse she has just drawn within her claws. I saw it all then with a quick flash of intuition. I had partly guessed it before, but now I was sure of it.

My poor Max, so brave and cheery and

patient! But she should not torment him any longer in my presence. If he had to suffer— and the cause of that suffering was still a mystery to me—she should not spy out his weakness. He had turned his face aside with a quick look of pain as he spoke, and the next moment I had mounted the breach and was begging Miss Darrell to assist me in the case of a poor family—old hospital acquaintances of mine who were emigrating to New Zealand.

My importunity seemed to surprise her. My sudden loquacity was an interruption, but I would not be repressed or silenced. I took the chair beside her, and made her look at me. I fixed her wandering attention and pressed her until she grew irritable with impatience. I saw Max was recovering himself; by-and-by he gave a forced laugh.

'You will have to give in, Miss Darrell. Ursula always gets her own way. How much do you want, child? You must be merciful to a poor vicar. Will that satisfy you?' offering me a sovereign, and Miss Darrell, after a moment's hesitation, produced the same sum from her purse.

I took her money coolly, but I would not resign the reins of the conversation any more into her hands. When Mr. Hamilton entered the room he stopped and looked at me with visible astonishment, he had never heard me so fluent before, but somehow my eloquence died a natural death after his entrance. I was still a little shy with Mr. Hamilton.

His manner was unusually genial this afternoon. I was sure he was delighted to see us both there again; he spoke to Max in a jesting tone, and then looked benignly at his cousin who was superintending the tea-table. She certainly looked uncommonly well that day; her dress of dark maroon cashmere and velvet fitted her fine figure exquisitely; her white well-shaped hands were, as usual, loaded with brilliant rings. She was a woman who needed ornaments—they would have looked lavish on any one else, they suited her admirably. Once I caught her looking with marked disfavour on my black serge dress; the pearl hoop that had been my mother's keeper was my sole adornment. I daresay she thought me extremely dowdy. I once heard her say in a pointed manner 'that her cousin Giles liked to see his women-folk well dressed; he was very fastidious on that point, and exceedingly hard to please.'

Mr. Hamilton seemed in the best of humours. I do not think that he remarked how very quiet Max was all tea-time. He pressed us to remain to dinner, and wanted to send off a message to the Vicarage; but we were neither of us to be persuaded, though Miss Darrell joined her entreaties to her cousin's.

I was anxious to leave the house as quickly as possible, and I knew by instinct what Max's feelings must be. I could not enjoy Mr. Hamilton's conversation, amusing as it was. I wanted to be alone with Max; I felt I could keep silence with him no longer. But we could not get rid of Mr. Hamilton; as we rose to take our departure he coolly announced his intention of walking with us.

'The Tylcotes have sent for me again,' he said casually. 'I may as well walk down with you now.' He looked at me as he spoke, but I am afraid my manner disappointed him; for once Mr. Hamilton was decidedly *de trop*. I am sure he must have noticed my hesitation, but it made no difference to his purpose. I had found out by this time that when Mr. Hamilton had made up his mind to do a certain thing, other people's moods did not influence him in the least; he half smiled as he went out to put on his great-coat, and as though he intended to punish me for my want of courtesy he talked to Max the whole time—not that I minded it in the least, only it was just his lordly way.

To my great relief, however, he left us as soon as we reached the Vicarage, so I wished him good-night quite amiably, and of course Max walked on with me to the cottage.

He was actually leaving me at the gate without a word except 'Good-night, Ursula,' but I laid my hand on his arm.

'You must come in, Max. I want to speak to you.'

'Not to-night, my dear,' he returned hurriedly. 'I have business letters to write before dinner.'

'They must wait then,' I replied decidedly, 'for I certainly do not intend to let you leave me just yet; don't be stubborn, Max, for you

know I always get my own way. Come in, I
want to tell you why Gladys never writes to
her brother.'   And he followed me into the
house without a word.

CHAPTER XXVII.

MAX OPENS HIS HEART.

BUT I did not at once join Max in the parlour, though he was evidently expecting me to do so; instead of that I ran upstairs to take off my walking things. It would be better to leave him alone a few minutes. When I returned he was leaning back in the easy-chair, with his hands clasped behind his head, evidently absorbed in thought. I was struck by his expression—it was that of a man who was nerving himself to bear some great trouble; there was a quiet, hopeless look on his face that touched me exceedingly. I took the chair opposite him, and waited for him to speak. He did not change his attitude when he saw me, but he looked at me gravely, and said, 'Well, Ursula,' but there was no interest in his tone.

Of course I knew what he meant, but I let that pass, and something seemed to choke my voice as I tried to answer him.

'Never mind that now—we will come to that presently. I want to tell you that I know it now, Max. I guessed a little of it before, but now I am sure of it.'

I had roused him effectually. A sort of dusky red came to his face as he sat up and looked at me; he did not ask me what I meant —we understood each other in a moment. He only sighed heavily, and said, 'I have never told you anything, Ursula, have I?' but his manner testified no displeasure. He would never have spoken a word to me of his own accord, and yet my sympathy would be a relief to him. I knew Max's nature so well: he was a shy, reticent man—he could not speak easily of his own feelings unless the ice were broken for him.

'Max,' I pleaded, and the tears came into my eyes, 'if my dear mother were living you would have told her all without reserve.'

'I should not have needed to tell her; she would have guessed it, Ursula. Poor Emmie, I never could keep anything from her. I have often told you you are like her ; you reminded me of her this afternoon.'

'Then you must make me your confidante in her stead. Do not refuse me again, Max ; I have asked this before. In spite of our strange relationship, we are still like brother and sister. You know how quickly I guessed Charlie's secret ; surely you can speak to me, who am her friend, of your affection for Gladys.'

I saw him shrink a little at that, and his honest brown eyes were full of pain.

'My affection for Gladys,' he repeated in a low voice. 'You are very frank, Ursula ; but somehow I do not seem to mind it. I never care for Miss Darrell to speak to me on the subject, although she has been so kind ; in fact no one could have been kinder—we can only act up to our own natures ; it is certainly not her fault, but only my misfortune that her sympathy jars on me.'

Max's words gave me acute pain.

'Surely you have not chosen Miss Darrell for your confidante, Max ? '

'I have chosen no one,' he returned, with gentle rebuke at my vehemence. 'Circumstances made Miss Darrell acquainted with my unlucky attachment. She did all she could to help me, and out of common gratitude I could not refuse to listen to her well-meant efforts to comfort me.'

I remained silent from sheer dismay ; things were far worse than I had imagined. I began to lose hope from the moment I heard Miss Darrell had been mixed up in the affair ; the thought sickened me. I could hardly bear to hear Max speak, and yet how was I to help him unless he made me acquainted with the real state of the case !

'I suppose I had better tell you all from the beginning,' he said rather dejectedly ; 'that is, as far as I know myself, for I can hardly tell you when I began to love Gladys, —I call her Gladys to myself,' with a faint smile—' and it comes naturally to me. I ought to have said Miss Hamilton.'

' But not to me, Max,' I returned eagerly.

' What does it matter what I call her ; she will never take the only name I want to give her ! ' was the melancholy reply to this. ' I only know one thing, Ursula, that for three years—ay, and longer than that—she has been the one woman in the world to me, and that as long as she and I live no other woman shall ever cross the threshold of the Vicarage as its mistress.'

'Has it gone so deep as that, my poor Max?'

'Yes,' he returned briefly; 'but we need not enter into that part of the subject; a man had best keep his own counsel in such matters. I want to tell you bare facts, Ursula; we may as well leave feelings alone. If you can help me to understand one or two points that are still misty to my comprehension, you will do me good service.'

'I will try my very best for you both.'

'Thank you, but we cannot both be helped in the same way; our paths do not lie together. Miss Hamilton has refused to become my wife.'

'Oh, Max! not refused, surely.' This was another blow—that he should have tried and failed—that Gladys with her own lips should have refused him; but perhaps he had written to her, and there was some misunderstanding; but when I hinted this to Max he shook his head.

'We cannot misunderstand a person's words.

Oh yes, I spoke to her, and she answered me; but I must not tell you things in this desultory fashion, or you will never understand. I have told you that I do not know when my attachment to Miss Hamilton commenced. It was gradual and imperceptible at first—very real, no doubt; but it had not mastered my reason. I always admired her, how could I help it?' with some emotion—' even you, who are not her lover, have owned to me that she is a beautiful creature. I suppose her beauty attracted me first until I saw the sweetness and unselfishness of her nature, and from that moment I lost my heart.

'The full consciousness came to me at the time of their trouble about Eric. I had been fond of the poor fellow, for his own sake as well as hers, but I never disguised his faults from her. I often told her that I feared for Eric's future; he had no ballast, it wanted a moral earthquake to steady him, and that it was no wonder that his caprices and extravagant moods angered his brother. She used to be half offended with me for my plain speaking, but she was too gentle to resent it, and she would beg me to use my influence with

Hamilton to entreat him not to be so hard on Eric.

'When the blow came, I was always up at Gladwyn—once, sometimes twice, a day; they all wanted me; it was my duty to be their consoler. I am glad to remember now that I was some comfort to her.'

'Wait a moment, Max; I must ask you something. Do you believe that Eric was guilty?'

'I am almost sorry that you have put that question,' he returned reluctantly. 'I never would tell her what I thought—it was all a mystery. Eric might have been tempted—it was not for me to say. She could see I was doubtful. I told her that if he were sinned against or sinning, our only thought should be to bring him back and reconcile him to his brother. "God will prove his innocence if he be blackened falsely," I said to her, and strange to say she forgave me my doubts.'

'Oh, Max, I see what you think.'

'How can I help it?' he replied, 'knowing Eric's character so well—he was so weak and impulsive—so easily led astray, and then he was under bad influences; you will have heard

Edgar Brown's name. He was a wild, dissipated fellow, and Hamilton had a right to forbid the acquaintance; both he and I knew that Edgar had low propensities, and was always lounging about public-houses with a set of loafers like himself. He has got worse since then, and has nearly broken his mother's heart. Do you think any man with a sense of responsibility would permit a youth of Eric's age to have such a friend? Yet this was a standing grievance with Eric, and I am sorry to say his sister took Edgar's part. Of course she knew no better—innocence is credulous—and Edgar was a sprightly, good-looking fellow, the sort that women never fail to pet.'

'Yes, I see; Eric was certainly to blame in this.'

'He was faulty on many more points. I am afraid, Ursula, you have been somewhat biassed by Miss Hamilton. You must remember that she idolised Eric; that she was blind to many of his faults; she made excuses for him, whenever it was possible to do so, but with all her weak partiality she could not deny that he was thriftless, idle, and extravagant; that he defied his brother's authority; that he even forgot himself so far as to use bad language in his presence. I believe, once, he even struck him, only Hamilton declared he had been drinking, so he merely turned him out of the room.'

I looked at Max sadly. 'This may be all true ; but I cannot believe that he took that cheque.'

'The circumstantial evidence against him is very strong,' he replied quietly. 'You do not know what power a sudden temptation has over these weak natures ; he was hard pressed, remember that ; he had gambling debts, thanks to Edgar. Fancy gambling debts at twenty ! I have tried to take Miss Hamilton's view of the case, but I cannot bring myself to believe in his innocence. Most likely he repented the moment he had done it, poor boy. Eric was no hardened sinner. I sometimes fear—at least, the terrible thought has crossed my mind, and 1 know Hamilton has had it too—that in his despair he might have made away with himself.'

'Oh, Max, this is too horrible !' and I shuddered as I thought of the beautiful young face so like Gladys', with its bright frank look that seemed to appeal to one's heart.

'Well, well, we need not speak of it ; but it

was a sad time for all of us—and yet in some ways it was a happy time to me. It was such a comfort to feel that I was necessary to them all; that they looked for me daily; that they could not do without me. I used to be with Hamilton every evening; and when Gladys was very ill they sent for me, because they said no one knew how to soothe her so well.

'Do you wonder, Ursula, that seeing her in her weakness and sorrow, she grew daily into my life, that my one thought was how I could help and comfort her?

'She was very gentle and submissive, and followed my advice in everything. When I told her that only work could cure her sore heart she did not contradict me; in a little while I had to check her feverish activity. She had overwhelmed herself with duties; she managed our mothers' meetings with Miss Darrell's help, taught in our schools, and helped train the choir. I had allotted her a district, and she worked it admirably. She was my right hand in everything; all the poor people worshipped her.'

'Yes, Max,' for he paused as though overwhelmed with some bitter sweet recollection.

'I loved her more each day, but I respected her sorrow, and tried to hide my feelings from her. It was more than a year after Eric's disappearance before I ventured to speak, and then it was by Hamilton's advice that I did so. He had set his heart on the match. He told me more than once that he would rather have me as a brother-in-law than any other man.

'I thought I had prepared her sufficiently, but it seems that she was very much startled by my proposal. Her trouble had so engrossed her that she had been perfectly blind to my meaning. It was all in vain, Ursula, for she did not love me—at least not in the right way. She told me so with tears, accusing herself of unkindness. She liked, most certainly she liked me, but perhaps she knew me too well.

'She was so unhappy at the thought of giving me pain—so sweet and gentle in her efforts to console me and heal the wound she had inflicted, that I could not lose hope. She told me that though she had trusted me entirely as her friend, she had never thought of me as her lover, and the idea was strange to her. This thought

gave me courage, and I begged that I might
be allowed to speak to her again at some future
time.

'She wanted to refuse, and said hurriedly
that she never intended to marry. But I took
these words as meaning nothing. A girl will
tell you this and believe it as she says it. I
suppose I pressed her hard to leave me this
margin of hope, for after reflecting a few
minutes she looked at me gravely and said it
should be as I wished. In a year's time I
might speak to her again, and she would know
her own mind.

'I pleaded for a shorter ordeal, though
secretly I was overjoyed at this crumb of
consolation vouchsafed to me. But she was
inexorable, though perfectly gentle in her
manner.

' " I wish you had set your heart on some one
else, Mr. Cunliffe," she said with a melancholy
smile, " for I can give you so little satisfaction.
I feel so confused and weary, as though life
afforded me no pleasure. But, indeed, I do all
you tell me, and I mean to go on with my
work."

' I was glad to hear her say this, for at least

I should have the happiness of seeing her every day.

' " In a year's time," she went on, " my heart may feel a little less heavy, and I shall have had opportunity to reflect over your words. I cannot tell you what my answer may be, but if you are wise you will not hope. If you do not come to me then, I shall know that you have changed, and shall not blame you in the least. You are free to choose any one else. I have so little encouragement to give you that I shall not expect you to submit to this ordeal." But I think her firmness was a little shaken, and she looked at me rather timidly when I thanked her very quietly and said that at the time appointed I would speak to her again. I supposed she had not realised the strength of my feelings.

' Ursula, I was by no means hopeless. And as the months passed on my hopes grew.

' I saw her daily, and after the first awkwardness had passed we were good friends. But her manner changed insensibly. She was less frank with me; at times she was almost shy. I saw her change colour when I looked at her. She was quiet in my presence, and yet my coming pleased her. I thought it would be well with me when the time came for renewing my suit, but it seems that I was a blind fool.

' I had put down the exact date, May 7th. It was last year, Ursula. I meant to adhere to the very day and hour, but before February closed my hopes had suffered eclipse.

' All at once Miss Hamilton's manner became cold and constrained, as you see it now. Her soft shyness, that had been so favourable a sign, disappeared entirely. She avoided me on every occasion. She seemed to fear to be alone with me a moment. Her nervousness was so visible and so distressing that I often left her in anger; a barrier—vague, and yet substantial— seemed built up between us.

' She began to neglect her work, and then to make excuses. She was overdone, and suffered from headache. The school work tired her. You have heard it all, Ursula; I need not repeat it.

' One by one she dropped her duties. The parish knew her no more. She certainly looked ill. Her melancholy increased. Something was evidently preying on her mind.

' One day Miss Darrell spoke to me. She

had been very kind, and had fed my hopes
all this time. But now she was the bearer of
bad news.

'She came to me in the study, while I was
waiting for Hamilton. She looked very pale
and discomposed, and asked if she might speak
to me. She was very unhappy about me, but
she did not think it right to let it go on. Gladys
wanted me to know. And then it all came
out.

'It could never be as I wished. Miss
Hamilton had been trying all this time to like
me, and once or twice she thought she had
succeeded, but the feeling had never lasted for
many days. I was not the right person. This
was the substance of Miss Darrell's explanation.

' " You know Gladys," she went on, " how
sensitive and affectionate her nature is; how
she hates to inflict pain. She is working herself up into a fever, at the thought that you
will speak to her again.

' " ' It was too terrible last time, Etta,' she
said to me, bursting into tears. 'I cannot
endure it again. How am I to tell him about
Claude ? ' "

' " About Claude ! " I almost shouted. Miss
Darrell looked frightened at my violence. She
shrank back, and turned still paler. I noticed
her hands trembled.

' " Oh, have you not noticed ? " she returned
feebly. " Oh ! what a cruel task this is, and
you are so good—so good."

' " Tell me what you mean ? " I replied
angrily, for I felt so savage at that moment that
a word of sympathy was more than I could
bear. You would not have known me at that
moment, Ursula. I am not easily roused, as
you know, but the blow was too sudden. I
must have forgotten myself to have spoken to
Miss Darrell in that tone. When I looked at
her, her mouth was quivering like a frightened
child's, and there were tears in her eyes.

' "I scarcely know that it is you," she faltered.
" Are men all like that when their wills are
crossed ? It is not my fault that you are hurt
in this way. And it is not Gladys' either. She
has tried—I am sure she has tried her hardest—
to bring herself to accede to your wishes. But
a woman cannot always regulate her own
heart."

' " You have mentioned Captain Hamilton's

name," I returned coldly, for her words seemed
only to aggravate and widen the sore. " Perhaps you will kindly explain what he has to do
with the matter?"

'She hesitated, and looked at me in a
pleading manner. I saw that she did not wish
to speak, but for once I was inexorable.

' " I must rely upon your honour, then, not
to repeat my words either to Giles or Gladys.
Your doing so would bring Gladys into trouble,
and after all there is nothing definitely settled."
I nodded assent to this, and she went on rather
reluctantly:

' " Claude was always fond of Gladys, but
we never knew how much he admired her until
he went away. They are only half-cousins—
Gladys' father was step-brother to Claude's.
Giles has always been averse to cousins marry-
ing, but we thought this would make a
difference."

' " They are engaged, then?" I asked, in a
loud voice, that seemed to startle Miss Darrell.

' " Oh, no, no," she returned eagerly, " there
is no engagement at all. Claude writes to her,
and she answers him, and I think he is making
way with her; she has owned as much to me.

Gladys is not one to talk of her feelings, especially on this subject; but it is easy to see how absorbed she is in those Indian letters, she is always brighter and more like herself when she has heard from Claude."

'" I am to deduce from all this that you believe Captain Hamilton has a better chance of winning her affections than I?"

' Again she hesitated, then drew a foreign letter slowly from her pocket. "I think I must read you a sentence from his last letter—he often writes to me as well as to Gladys. Yes, here it is: 'Your last letter has been a great comfort to me, my dear Etta—it was more than a poor fellow had a right to expect. I do believe that this long absence has served my purpose, and the scratch I got at Singapore. Girls are curious creatures; one never can tell how to tackle them, and my special cousin knows how to keep one at a distance, but I begin to feel I am making way at last. She wrote to me very sweetly last mail. I carry that letter everywhere; there was a sweetness about it that gave me hope. If I can get leave—though Heaven knows when that will be—I mean to come home and carry the breach boldly. I shall first show her my wound and my medal, and then throw myself at her pretty little feet. Gladys——' No, I must not read any more; you see how it is, Mr. Cunliffe?"

'"Yes, I see how it is," I returned slowly. "Forgive me if I have been impatient or unmindful of your kindness," and then I took up my hat and left the room, and it was weeks before I set foot in Gladwyn again.'

'Oh, Max, my poor Max!' I returned stroking his hand softly. He did not take it away; he only looked at me with his kind smile.

'That was Emmie's way—her favourite little caress. Wait a moment, Ursula, my dear, I am going out for a breath of air,' and he stood in the porch for a few minutes looking up at the winter sky seamed with stars, and then came back to me quietly, and waited for me to speak.

CHAPTER XXVIII.

CROSSING THE RIVER.

AX waited for me to speak, but I had no words ready for the occasion. My silence seemed to perplex him.

'You have heard everything now, Ursula.'

'Yes, I suppose so. I am very sorry for you, Max; you have suffered cruelly. And this only happened last year?'

'Last February.'

'It is very strange—very mysterious; I do not seem to understand it. I cannot find the clue to all this.'

'There is no clue needed,' he returned impatiently. 'Miss Hamilton is in love with her cousin, and is sorry for my disappointment.'

I do not believe it,' I replied bluntly; and yet, as I said this, Gladys' conduct seemed to me perfectly inexplicable. It was just possible that Max's statement, after all, might be correct, that she did not love him well enough to marry him; and this would account for her nervousness and constraint in his presence—a sensitive girl like Gladys would never be at her ease under such circumstances. But she had promised not to withdraw her friendship; why had she then given up her work and made herself a stranger to his dearest interest? I had seen her struggle with herself when he had begged her to resume her class. A brightness had come to her eyes, her manner had become warm and animated, as though the stirring of new life were in her veins, and then she had refused him very gently, and a certain dimness and blight had crept over her. I had wondered then at her.

No, I could not bring myself to believe that she was indifferent to Max. He was so good, so worthy of her. And yet—and yet do we women always choose the best? Perhaps, as Max said, she knew him too well for him to influence her fancy. Captain Hamilton's scars and medals might cast a gloom over her. Gladys was very impulsive and enthusiastic;

perhaps Max was too quiet and gentle to take
her heart by storm.

I had plenty of time for these reflections,
for Max sat moodily silent after my blunt remark, but at last he said—

'I am afraid I believe it, Ursula, and that
is more to the purpose. Miss Darrell has dis-
pelled my last hope.'

'You mean that Captain Hamilton's return
speaks badly for your chances?'

'I have no chances,' very gloomily. 'I am
out of the running. Miss Hamilton's message—
for I suppose it was a message—was my final
answer. She did not wish me to speak to
her again.'

'Are you sure that she sent that message?'

'Am I sure that I am sitting here?' he
answered rather irritably. 'What have you
got in your head, Ursula, my dear?—you must
not let personal dislike influence your better
judgment. Perhaps Miss Darrell is not to my
taste; I think her sometimes officious and
wanting in delicacy; but I do not doubt her
for a moment.'

'That is a pity,' I returned dryly, 'for she
is certainly not true; but all you men swear by

her,' for I felt—Heaven forgive me!—almost a hatred of this woman, unreasonable as it seemed; but women have these instincts sometimes, and Max had warned me against Miss Darrell from the first.

'I will be frank with you,' I continued more quietly. 'I do not read between the lines—in other words, I do not understand Gladys' behaviour. It may be as you say—I do not wish to delude you with false hopes, my poor Max; Gladys may care more for Captain Hamilton than she does for you; but it seems to me that you acted wrongly on one point—you meant it for the best—but you ought to have spoken to Gladys yourself.'

'I wonder that you should say that, Ursula,' he returned in rather a hurt voice. 'I may be weak about Miss Hamilton, but I am hardly as weak as that. Do you think me capable of persecuting the woman I love?'

'It would not be persecution,' I replied firmly, for I was determined to speak my mind on this point. 'Miss Darrell may have misconstrued her meaning, the truth loses by repetition—she may have added to or diminished her words. A third person should never be mixed

up in a love affair; trouble always comes of
it. I think you were wrong, Max—you let
yourself be managed by Miss Darrell; she has
nothing to do with you or Gladys.'

'I could not help it if she came to me.'

'True, she thrust herself in between you;
well, it is too late to speak of that now. If you
will take my advice, Max,' for the thought had
come upon me like a flash of inspiration, 'you
will go down to Bournemouth and speak to
Gladys, keeping your own counsel and telling
no one of your intention.'

I saw Max stare at me as though he thought
I had lost my senses, and then a sudden light
came into his eyes.

'You will go down to Bournemouth,' I went
on, 'and the Maberleys will be glad to see you;
you are an old friend, and they will ask no
questions and think no ill. You will have no
difficulty in seeing Gladys alone; speak to her
promptly and frankly, ask her what her behaviour has meant, and if she really prefers her
cousin. If you must know the worst, it will be
better to know it now, and from her own lips.
Do go, Max, like a brave man.' But even before
I finished speaking, the light had died out of

his eyes, and his manner had resumed its old sadness.

'No, Ursula; you mean well, but it will not do. I cannot persecute her in this way; Captain Hamilton is coming home in July, she has given him permission to come. I will wait for that—I shall very soon see how matters stand between them. I shall only need to see her with him; probably I shall not speak to her at all.'

I could have wrung my hands over Max's obstinacy and Quixotism—he carried his generosity to a fault—few men would be so patient and forbearing.

How could he stand aside hopelessly and let another man win his prize? But perhaps he considered it was already won. I pleaded with him again. I even went so far as to contradict my theory about a third person, and offered to sound Gladys about her cousin, but he silenced me peremptorily.

'Promise me that you will do nothing of the kind; give me your word of honour, Ursula, that you will respect my confidence. Good heavens! if I thought that you would betray me, and to her of all people, I should indeed bitterly repent my trust in you.'

Max was so agitated, he spoke so angrily, that I hastened to soothe him. Of course his confidence was sacred; how could he think such things of me?—I was not like Miss—— but here I pulled myself up. He might be as blind and foolish as he liked, he might commit suicide, and I would not hinder him; he should enjoy his misery in his own way—and more to that effect.

'Now I have made you cross, little she-bear,' he said, laying his hand on mine, 'and you have been so patient and have given my woes such a comfortable hearing. You frightened me for a moment, for I know how quick and impulsive you can be. No, no, my dear. I hold you to your own words, a third person must not be mixed up in a love affair, it only brings trouble.'

'You have proved the truth of my words,' I remarked coolly. 'Very well, I suppose I must forgive you; only never do it again, on your peril; you know I am to be trusted.'

'To be sure, you are as true as steel, Ursula.'

'Very well then, in that case you have nothing to fear. I will be wise and wary for your sake, and guard your honour sacredly as my own; if I can give you a gleam of hope I will—anyhow I shall watch.'

'Thank you, dear; and now we will not talk any more about it—now you know why I wanted you to be her friend. I am glad to think she is so fond of you.' But I would not let him change the subject just yet.

'Max,' I said, detaining him, for he rose to go, 'all this is dreadfully hard for you. Shall you go away—if—if—this happens?'

'No,' he returned quietly, 'it is they who will go away. Captain Hamilton cannot leave his regiment, he is far too fond of an active life. It will be dreary enough, God knows, but it will not be harder than the life I have led these twelve months, trying to win her back to her work, and to put myself in the background. It has worn me out, Ursula. I could not stand that sort of thing much longer, it is a relief to me that she is away.'

'Yes, I can understand this.'

'It makes one think after all that the extreme party have something in their argument in favour of the celibacy of the clergy. Not that I hold with them, for all that; but all this sort thing takes the heart out of a man and comes between him and his work. I should be a better priest if I were a happier man, Ursula.'

'I doubt that, Max,' and the tears rose to my eyes, for I knew how good he was, and what a friend to his people.

'My dear, I differ from you. I believe there is no work like happy work—work done by a heart at leisure from itself; but of course we clergy and laity must take what Heaven sends us.' And then he held out his hands to me, and I suppose he saw how unhappy I was for his sake.

'Don't fret about me, my dear little Ursula,' he said kindly. 'The back gets fitted for the burden, and by this time I have grown accustomed to my pain; it will all be right some day—I shall not be blamed up there for loving her,' and he left me with a smile.

I passed a miserable evening thinking of Max. Next to Charlie he had been my closest friend from girlhood; I had been accustomed to look to him for advice in all my difficulties, to rely upon his counsel. I knew that people who were comparatively strangers to him thought he was almost too easy-going, and a little weak from excess of good-nature. He was too tolerant of other folk's failings, they said; he preached mercy where severity would be more bracing and wholesome; and no doubt they thought that he judged himself as leniently—but they did not know Max.

I never knew a man harder to himself. Charitable to others, he had no self-pity; selfish aims were impossible to him. He who could not endure to witness even a child or animal suffer, would have plucked out his right eye or parted with his right hand, in Gospel phrase, if by doing so he could witness to the truth, or spare pain to a weaker human being. It was this knowledge of his inner life that made Max so priestly in my eyes. I knew he was pure enough and strong enough to meet even Gladys' demands—nothing but a modern Bayard would ever satisfy her fastidious taste; she would not look on a man's statue, or his outward beauty—such things would seem paltry to her; but he who aspired to be her lord and master must be worthy of all reverence and must have won his spurs; so much had I learnt from my friendship with Gladys.

I pondered over Max's words, and tried to piece the fragments of our conversation with recollections of my talks with Gladys. I recalled much that had passed. I endeavoured to find the clue to her downcast, troubled looks, her quenched and listless manner. I felt dimly that some strange misunderstanding wrapped these two in a close fog. What had brought about this chill murky atmosphere, in which they failed to recognise each other's meaning? This was the mystery—lives had often been shipwrecked from these miserable misunderstandings, for want of a word. I felt completely baffled, and before the evening was over I could have cried with the sense of utter failure and bewilderment. If Max's chivalrous scruples had not tied my hands, I would have gone to Gladys boldly, and asked her what it all meant; I would have challenged her truth—I would have compelled her to answer me; but I dare not break my promise. By letter and in the spirit I would respect Max's wishes.

But I resolved to watch; no eyes should be so vigilant as mine. I was determined that nothing should escape my scrutiny; at least I was in possession of certain facts that would help me in finding the clue I wanted. I knew now that Max loved Gladys, and had tried to win her; that he had nearly done so was also evident. What had wrought that sudden change? Had Captain Hamilton's brilliant successes really dazzled her fancy and blinded her to Max's quiet unobtrusive virtues; did she really and truly prefer her cousin? This was what I had to find out, and here Max could not help me.

There was one thing I was glad to know, that Mr. Hamilton favoured Max's suit, at least I should not be working against him. I do not know why, but the thought of doing so would have pained me; I no longer wished to array myself for war against Mr. Hamilton; my enmity had died a natural death for want of fuel.

I felt grateful to him for his kindness to Max; no doubt he had a fellow-feeling with him. That dear old gossip, Mrs. Maberley, had told me something about Mr. Hamilton on my second visit that had made me feel very sorry for him. Max knew about it, of course—he had said a word to me once on the subject, but it was not Max's way to gossip about his neigh-

bours; he once said laughing that he left all
the choice bits of scandal to his good old friend
at Maplehurst.

It was from Mrs. Maberley that I heard
all about Mr. Hamilton's disappointment, and
why he had not married. When he was about
eight and twenty he had been engaged to a
young widow.

'She was a beautiful creature, my dear,'
observed the old lady; 'the Colonel said he
had never seen a handsomer woman. She was
an Irish beauty, and had those wonderful grey
eyes and dark eyelashes that make you
wonder what colour they are, and she had the
sweetest smile possible; any man would have
been bewitched by it. I never saw a young
man more in love than Giles—when he came
here he could talk of nothing but Mrs. Carrick :
her name was Ella, I remember. Well, it went
on for some months, and he was preparing
for the wedding; there was to be a nursery got
ready, for she had one little boy, and Giles
already doted on the child, when all at once
there came a letter from his lady-love—and a
very pretty letter it was. Giles must forgive
her, it said, she was utterly wretched at the

thought of the pain she was giving him, but she was mistaken in the strength of her attachment. She had come to the conclusion that they would not be happy together, that in fact she preferred some one else.

' She did not mention that this other lover was richer than Giles and had a title, but of course he found out that this was the case. The fickle Irish beauty had caught the fancy of an elderly English nobleman, with a large family of grown-up sons and daughters. My dear, it was a very heartless piece of work—it changed Giles completely; he never spoke about it to any one, but if ever a man was heart-broken, Giles was—he was never the same after that; it made him hard and bitter; he is always railing against women, or saying disagreeable home-truths about them. And of course Mrs. Carrick, or rather Lady Howe, is to blame for that. Oh, my dear, she may deck herself with diamonds, as they say she does, and call herself happy—which she is not, with a gouty, ill-tempered old husband who is jealous of her—but I'll be bound she thinks of Giles sometimes with regret, and scorns herself for her folly.'

Poor Mr. Hamilton! And this had all happened about six or seven years ago—no wonder he looked stern and said bitter things. He was not naturally sweet-tempered, like Max; such a misfortune would sour him.

'Ah, well,' I said to myself as I went up to bed, 'it is perfectly true what Longfellow says, "Into each life some rain must fall, some days must be dark and gloomy;" but it is strange that they both have suffered. It is a good thing, perhaps, that such an experience is never likely to happen to me. There is some consolation to be deduced even from my want of beauty: no man will fall in love with me, and then play me false;' and with that a curious feeling came over me, a sudden inexplicable sense of want and loneliness, something I could not define, that took no definite shape and had no similitude, and yet haunted me with a sense of ill; but the next moment I was struggling fiercely with the unknown and unwelcome guest.

'For shame,' I said to myself, 'this is weakness and pure selfishness, mere sentimental feverishness; this is not like the strong-minded young person Miss Darrell calls me. What if loneliness be appointed me?—we must each

have our cross. Perhaps, as life goes on and
I grow older, it may be a little hard to bear
at times, but my loneliness would be better
than the sort of pain Mr. Hamilton and Max
have endured.' And as I thought this a sudden
conviction came to me that I could not have
borne a like fate, a dim instinct that told me
that I should suffer keenly and long—that it
would be better, far better, that the deepest
instincts of my woman's nature should never be
roused than be kindled only to die away into
ashes, as many women's affections have been
suffered to die. 'Anything but that,' I said to
myself, with a sudden thrill of pain that surprised me with its intensity.

All this time through the long cold weeks
Elspeth had been slowly dying. Quietly and
gradually the blind woman's strength had
ebbed and lessened, until early in March we
knew she could not last much longer.

She suffered no pain and uttered no com-
plaint. She lay peacefully propped up with
pillows on the bed where Mary Marshall had
breathed her last, and her pale wrinkled face
grew almost as white as the cap border that
encircled it.

At the commencement of her illness I was unable to be much with her. Susan and Phebe Locke had thoroughly engrossed me, and a hurried visit morning and evening to give Peggy orders was all that was possible under the circumstances ; but I saw that she was well cared for and comfortable, and Peggy was very good to her and kept the children out of the room.

'Ay, my bairn, I am dying like a lady,' she said to me one day, 'and it is good to be here on poor Mary's bed. See the fine clean sheets that Peggy has put me on, and the grand quilt that keeps my feet warm ! Sometimes I could cry with the comfort of it all; and there is the broth and the jelly always ready ; and what can a poor old body want more ? '

When Susan was convalescent I spent more time with Elspeth. I knew she loved to have me beside her, and to listen to the chapters and Psalms I read to her. She would ask me to sing to her sometimes, and often we would sit and talk of the days that seemed so 'few and evil' in the light of advancing immortality.

'Ay, dearie,' she would say, 'it is not much to look back upon except in an angel's

sight—a poor old woman's life, who worked
and struggled to keep her master and children
from clemming. I used to think it hard sometimes that I could not get to church on Sunday
morning—for I was aye a woman for church—
but I had to stand at my wash-tub often until
late on Saturday night.   " After a day's charing,
rinsing out the children's bits of things, and
ironing them too, how is a poor tired body like
me to get religion? " I would say sometimes
when I was fairly moithered with it all.   But,
Miss Garston, my dear, I'm glad, as I lie here,
to know that I never neglected the children
God had given me ; and so He took care of all
that ; He knew when I was too tired to put up
a prayer that it was not for the want of loving
Him.'

'No, indeed, Elspeth. I often think we
ought not to be too hard on poor people.'

'That's true,' brightening up visibly. 'He
is no severe taskmaster demanding bricks out
of stubble ; He knows poor labouring people
are often tired and out of heart. I used to say
to my master sometimes, " Ah, well, we must
leave all that for heaven ; we shall have a fine
rest there, and plenty of time to sing our hymns

and talk to the Lord Jesus. He was a labouring Man too, and He will know all about it."
I often comforted my master like that.'

Elspeth's quaint talk interested me greatly
I grew to love her dearly, and I liked to feel
that she was fond of me in return. I could
have sat by her contentedly for hours, holding
her hard work-worn hand and listening to her
gentle flow of talk with its Scriptural phrases
and simple realistic thoughts. It was like
washing some pilgrim's feet at a feast to listen
to Elspeth.

One evening she told me that she had been
thinking of me.

'I wanted to know what you were like,
my bairn,' she said with her pretty Scotch
accent; 'and the doctor came in as I was
turning it over in my mind, so I made bold to
ask him to describe you. I thought he was a
long time answering, and at last he said—

' "What put that into your head, Granny?"
as if he were a little bit taken aback by the
question.

' "Well, doctor," I returned, "we all of us
like to see the faces of those we love; and I
am all in the dark. That dear young lady is

doing the Lord's work with all her might, and
she has a voice that makes me think of heaven,
and the choirs of angels, and the golden harps,
and maybe her face is as beautiful as her voice."

' "Oh no," he says quite sharply to that,
" she is not beautiful at all; indeed, I am not
sure that most people would not think her
plain."

'I suppose I was an old ninny, but I did
not like to hear him say this, my bairn, for I
knew it could not be the truth; but he went
on after a minute—

' " It is not easy to describe the face of a
person one knows so well. I find it difficult to
answer your question. Miss Garston has such
a true face, one seems to trust it in a minute;
it is the face of an honest kindly woman who
will never do you any harm; " and then I
saw what he meant. Why, bairn, the angels
have this sort of beauty, and it lasts the
longest; that is the sort of face they have
there.'

I heard all this silently, and was thankful
that Elspeth's blind eyes could not see the
burning flush of mortification that rose to my
face. The dear garrulous old body, how could

she have put such a question to Mr. Hamilton;
and yet how kindly he had answered. 'A
sudden recollection of Irish dark grey eyes
with black lashes came to my mind; I knew
Mr. Hamilton was a connoisseur of beauty. I
had often heard him describe people, and point
out their physical defects with the keenest
criticism—he was singularly fastidious on this
point; but in spite of my humiliation I was
glad to know that he had spoken so gently. He
had told the truth simply, that was all—at
least he had owned I was true—I must content
myself with this tribute to my honesty.

But it was some days before I could recall
Elspeth's words without a sensation of prickly
heat; it is strange how painfully these little pin-
pricks to our vanity affect us. I was angry
with myself for remembering them, and yet
they rankled, in spite of Elspeth's quaint and
homely consolation—alas! I was not better
than my fellows—Ursula Garston was not the
strong-minded woman that Miss Darrell called
her.

But when I next met Mr. Hamilton, I had
other thoughts to engross me, for Elspeth was
dying, and we were standing together by her

bedside. I had not sent for Mr. Hamilton, for
I knew that he could do nothing more for her;
but he had met one of the children in the
village, and on hearing the end was approaching had come at once to render me any help in
his power—perhaps he thought I should like
to have him there:

Elspeth's pinched wrinkled face brightened
as she heard his voice. 'Ay, doctor, I am glad
to know you are there; you have been nought
but kind to me all these years, and now thanks
to this bairn I am dying like a lady. The
Lord bless you both—and He will—He will!'
with feeble earnestness.

I bent down and kissed her cold cheek.
'Never mind us, Elspeth, only tell us that all
is well with you—you are not afraid, dear
Granny?'

'What's to fear, my bairn, with the Lord
holding my hand—and He will not let go—ah,
no, He will never let go! Ay, I have come to
the dark river, but it will not do more than
wet my feet. I'll be carried over, for I am old
and weak—old and weak, my dearie.' These
were her last words, and half an hour afterwards the change came, and Elspeth's sight-

less eyes were opened to the light of immortality!

That night I took up a little worn copy of the 'Pilgrim's Progress' that I had had from childhood, and opened it at a favourite passage, where Christian and his companion are talking with the shining ones as they went up toward the Celestial city, and I thought of Elspeth as I read it. 'You are going now,' said they, 'to the paradise of God, wherein you shall see the Tree of Life, and eat of the never-failing fruit thereof; and when you come there you shall have white robes given you, and your walk and talk shall be every day with the King, even all the days of eternity. There you shall not see again such things as you saw when you were in the lower regions, upon the earth, to wit, sorrow, sickness, and death, for the former things are passed away. . . .

'And the men asked, what must we do in that Holy Place? To whom it was answered: " You must then receive the comfort of your toil, and have joy for all your sorrow."' I thought of Elspeth's last words, 'Old and weak, old and weak, my dearie.' Surely they had come true—

those aged feet had barely touched the cold water. Gently and tenderly she had been carried across to the green pastures and still waters in the Paradise of God.

CHAPTER XXIX.

MISS DARRELL HAS A HEADACHE.

I BEGAN to feel that Gladys had been away a long time, and to wish for her return. I was much disappointed then on receiving a letter from her about a fortnight after Elspeth's death, telling me that Colonel Maberley had made up his mind to spend Easter in Paris, and that she had promised to accompany them.

'I shall be sorry to be so long without your companionship,' she wrote. 'I miss you more than I can say, but I am sure that it is far better for me to remain away as long as possible; the change is certainly doing me good. I am quite strong and well; they spoil me dreadfully, but I think this sort of treatment suits me best.'

It was a long letter, and seemed to be written in a more cheerful mood than usual. There was a charming description of a trip they had taken, with little graceful touches of humour here and there.

I handed the letter silently to Max when he called the next day. I thought that it would be no harm to show it to him. He took it to the window, and was so busy reading it that I had half finished a letter I was writing to Jill before he at last laid it down on my desk.

'Thank you for letting me see it,' he said quietly, 'it has been a great pleasure. Somehow, as I read it, it seemed as though the old Gladys Hamilton had written it—not the one we know now. Indeed, she seems much better.'

'Yes, and we must make up our minds to do without her,' I answered with a sigh.

'And we shall do so most willingly,' he returned, with a sort of tacit rebuke to my selfishness, 'if we know the change is benefiting her.' And then, with a change of tone, 'What a beautiful handwriting hers is, Ursula, so firm and clear, so characteristic of the writer.

Does she often write you such long, interesting letters? You are much to be envied, my dear. Well, well, the day's work is waiting for me,' and with that he went off without saying another word.

My next visitor was Mr. Hamilton. He came to tell me of an accident case. A young labourer had fallen off a scaffolding, and a compound fracture of the right arm had been the result. He was also badly shaken and bruised, and was altogether in a miserable plight.

I promised, of course, to go to him at once; but he told me that there was no immediate hurry—he had attended to the arm and left him very comfortable, and he would do well for the next hour or two; and, as Mr. Hamilton seemed inclined to linger for a little chat, I could not refuse to oblige him.

'It is just as well that this piece of work has come to me,' I said presently, 'for I was feeling terribly idle. Since Elspeth's death I have not had a single case, and have employed my leisure in writing long letters to my relations and taking country rambles with Tinker.'

'That is right,' he returned heartily. 'I

am sure we worked you far too hard at one
time.'

'It did not hurt me, and I should not care
to be idle for long.—Yes, I have heard from
Gladys,' for his eyes fell on the open letter
that lay beside us. 'I am rather disappointed
that I shall not see her before I go away.'

'Are you going away, then?' he asked very
quickly, and I thought the news did not seem
to please him.

'Not for three weeks. I hope my patient
will be getting on by that time, and will be
able to spare me; at any rate, I can give his
mother a lesson or two. You know my cousin
is to be married, and I have promised to help
Aunt Philippa.'

'How long do you think you will be away?'
he demanded, with a touch of his old abruptness.

'For a fortnight. I could not arrange for
less. Sara is making such a point of it.'

'A whole fortnight! I am afraid you are
terribly idle after all, Miss Garston. You are
growing tired of this humdrum place. You
are yearning for "the leek and cucumbers
of Egypt,"' with a grim smile.

'You are wrong,' I returned, with more

earnestness than the occasion warranted. 'I feel a strange reluctance to re-enter Vanity Fair. The splendours of a gay wedding are not to my taste. Sara tells me that her reception after the ceremony will be attended by about two hundred guests. To me the idea is simply barbarous. I expect I shall be heartily glad to get back to Heathfield.'

I was surprised to see how pleased Mr. Hamilton looked at this speech. I had been thinking of my work and my quiet little parlour, not of Gladwyn, when I spoke; but he seemed to accept it as a personal compliment.

'I assure you that we shall welcome you back most gladly,' he returned. 'The place will not seem like itself without our busy village nurse. Well, you have worked hard enough for six months, you deserve a holiday. I should like to see you in your butterfly garb, Miss Garston. I fancy, however, that I should not recognise you.'

With a sudden pang I remembered Elspeth's words. He does not think that such home attire will become me. I thought he preferred me in my usual nun's garb of black serge.

'Oh,' I said petulantly and foolishly, 'I must own that I shall look rather like a crow dressed up in peacock's feathers in the grand gown Sara has chosen for me;' but I was a little taken aback, and felt inclined to laugh, when he asked me, with an air of interest, what it was like in colour and material.

'Sara wished it to be red plush,' I replied demurely; 'but I refused to wear it; so she has waived that in favour of a dark green velvet. I think it is absolutely wicked to make Uncle Brian pay for such a dress; but it seems that Sara will get her own way, so I must put up with all they choose to give me.'

'That is hardly spoken graciously. If your uncle be rich, why should he not please himself in buying you a velvet gown? I think the fair bride elect has good taste. You will look very well in dark green velvet—light tints would not suit you at all—red would be too gay.'

He spoke with such gravity and decision that I thought it best not to contradict him. I even repressed my inclination to laugh; if he liked to be dogmatic on the subject of my

dress, I would not hinder him ; the next moment, however, he dismissed the matter.

'I agree with you in disliking gay weddings,
the idea is singularly repugnant to me. Because
two people elect to join hands for the journey
of life, is there any adequate reason why all
their idle acquaintances should accompany them
with cymbals and prancings and all sorts of
fooleries just at the most solemn moment of
their life ? '

'I suppose they wish to express their sympathy,' I returned.

'Sympathy should wear a quieter garb.
These folks come to church to show their fine
feathers and make a fuss—they do not care a jot
for the solemnity of the service—and yet to me
it is as awful in its way as the burial service.
" Till death us do part "—can any one, man or
woman, say these words lightly and not bring
down a doom upon himself? He spoke with
suppressed excitement, walking up and down
the room—one could see how strongly he felt
his words. Was he thinking of Mrs. Carrick, I
wondered. He gave a slight shudder as though
some unwelcome thought obtruded itself, and
then he turned to me with a forced smile.

'I am boring you, I am afraid. I get horribly excited over the shams of conventionality—what were we talking about? Oh, I remember—Gladys' letter. Yes, she has written to Lady Betty, not such a volume as that,' glancing at the closely written sheets. 'You are her chief correspondent, I believe—but she told us her plans. For my part I am glad that she should enjoy this trip to Paris—really, the Maberleys are most kind. I sent her a cheque to add to her amusements, for of course all girls like shopping.'

How generous he was to his sisters; with all his faults of manner, he seemed to grudge them nothing. But all the same I knew Gladys would have valued a few kind words from him far more than the cheque; but perhaps he had written to her as well. But he seemed rather surprised when I asked him the question.

'Oh no, I never write to my sisters—they would not care for a letter from me. Etta offered to enclose it in a letter she had just finished to Gladys, so that saved all trouble. By the bye, Miss Garston, I hope you will come up to Gladwyn one evening before you leave

Heathfield. I do not see why we are to be deserted in this fashion.'

Neither did I, if he put it in this way; reluctant as I was to spend an evening there in Gladys' absence, it certainly was not quite kind either to him or Lady Betty to refuse. He seemed to anticipate a refusal, however, for he said hastily—

'Never mind answering me now. Etta shall write to you in proper form, and you shall fix your own evening. Now I have hindered you sufficiently, so I will take my leave,' which he did, but I heard him some time afterwards talking to Nathaniel in the porch.

A few days after this I received a civil little note from Miss Darrell, pressing me to spend a long evening with them, and begging me to bring my prettiest songs.

I made the rather lame excuse that I was much engaged with my new patient, and fixed the latest day that I could—the very last evening before I was to leave for London. Mr. Hamilton met me a few hours afterwards, and asked me rather dryly what my numerous engagements could be.

'You are the most unsociable of your sex,'

he added, when I had no answer to make to
this. 'I shall take care that you are properly
punished, for neither Cunliffe nor Tudor shall be
asked to meet you. Etta was sure you would
like one or both to come, but I put my veto on
it at once.'

'Then you were very disagreeable,' I returned laughingly. 'I wanted Uncle Max very
much,' but he only shook his head at me good-
humouredly, and scolded me for my want of
amiability.

I determined, when the evening came, that
he should not find fault with me in any way.
I was rather in holiday mood; my patient was
going on well, and his mother was a neat,
capable body, and might be trusted to look
after him. No other cases had come to me,
and I might leave Heathfield with a clear conscience. Uncle Max would miss me, but an old
college friend was coming to stay at the Vicarage, so I could be better spared. I had seen
a great deal of Mr. Tudor lately. I often met
him in the village, and he always turned back
and walked with me; he met me on this occasion, and walked to the gates of Gladwyn.
Indeed, he detained me for some minutes in

the road, trying to extract particulars about the wedding.

'Miss Jocelyn is to be bridesmaid, then,' describing a circle with his stick in the dust.

'Yes, poor Sara is afraid that she will be quite overshadowed by Jill's bigness; she has made her promise not to stand quite close. They have got a match for her. Grace Underley is as tall as Jill, and very fair. Sara calls them her night and morning bridesmaids.'

'I think I shall be in London on the fourteenth. I thought, Miss Garston, that there was a prejudice to weddings in May.'

'Yes; but Sara laughs at the idea, and Colonel Ferguson says it is all nonsense. I did not know you were coming to town so soon.'

'Some of my people will be up then,' he said absently; 'perhaps I shall have a peep at you all; but, of course,'—rather hastily—' I shall not call at Hyde Park Gate until the wedding is over.'

I wished he would not call then. What was the good of feeding his boyish fancy? it would soon die a natural death, if he would only be wise. Poor Mr. Tudor, I began to be afraid that he was very much in earnest after all; there was a grave expression on his face as he turned away. Perhaps he knew, as I did, that our big awkward Jill would develop into a splendid woman; that one of these days Jocelyn Garston would be far more admired than her sister—the ugly duckling would soon change into a swan. There were times even now when Jill looked positively handsome, if only her short black locks would grow, and she would leave off hunching her shoulders.

' I should like Lawrence Tudor to have my Jill, if he were only rich ; but there is no hope for him now, poor fellow,' I said to myself, as I walked up the gravel walk towards the house.

Gladwyn looked its best this evening. The shady little lawns that surrounded the house looked cool and inviting ; the birds were singing merrily from the avenue of young oaks ; the air was sweet with the scent of May blossoms and wallflowers—great bunches of them were placed in the hall.

Thornton, who admitted me, said that Leah would be waiting for me in the blue room, as Miss Darrell's room was called, so I went up at once.

I was passing through the dressing-room,

when I saw the bed-room door was half opened,
and a voice—I scarcely recognised it as
Miss Darrell's; it was so different to her usual
low toneless voice—exclaimed angrily, 'You
forget yourself strangely, Leah; one would
think you were the mistress and I the maid,
to hear you speaking to me.'

'I can't help that, Miss Etta,' returned the
woman, insolently. 'If you are not more
punctual in your payments, I will go to the
master myself and tell him.' But here I
knocked sharply at the door to warn them of
my presence, and Leah ceased abruptly, while
Miss Darrell bade me enter.

She tried to meet me as usual, but her face
was flushed, and she looked at me uneasily, as
though she feared that I had overheard Leah's
speech. I thought Leah looked sullen and
stolid as she waited upon me. It was a most
forbidding face. I was glad when Miss Darrell
dismissed her on some slight pretext.

'Leah is in a bad temper this evening,' she
observed, examining the clasp of a handsome
bracelet as she spoke. I noticed then that she
had beautiful arms, as well as finely shaped
hands, and the emerald-eyed snake showed to

advantage. 'She is a most invaluable person, but she can take liberties sometimes. Perhaps you heard me scolding her, but I consider she was decidedly in the wrong.'

'She does not look very good-tempered,' was my reply. Miss Darrell still looked flushed and perturbed; but she took up her fan and vinaigrette, and proposed that we should join Lady Betty in the drawing-room. Leah was in the hall. As we passed her, she addressed Miss Darrell—

'If you can spare me a moment, ma'am, I should like to speak to you,' she said quite civilly; but I thought her manner a little menacing.

'Will not another time do, Leah?' returned her mistress, in a worried tone; but the next moment she begged me to go in without her.

Lady Betty was sitting by the open window with Nap beside her. I thought the poor little girl looked dull and lonely. She gave an exclamation of pleasure at seeing me, and ran towards me with outstretched hands. She looked like a child in her little white gown and blue ribbons, with her short curly hair.

'I am so glad to see you, Miss Garston. I

thought Etta would keep you. I have been
alone all the afternoon—Etta never sits with
me now. How I wish Gladys would come
back. I have no one to speak to, and I miss
her horribly.'

'.Poor Lady Betty!'

'You would say so, if you knew how
horrid it all was. Just now, as I was sitting
alone, I felt like a poor little princess shut up
in an enchanted tower. Giles is the Magician,
and Etta is the wicked Witch. I was making
up quite a story about it.'

'Why have you not been to see me lately,
Lady Betty?'

'Oh, how silly you are to ask me such a
question,' she returned pettishly; 'you had
better ask Witch-Etta. Now you pretend
to look surprised—she won't let me come—
there.'

'My dear child, surely you need not con-
sult your cousin.'

'Of course not,' wrinkling her forehead;
'but then you see Witch-Etta consults me—
she makes a point of finding out all my little
plans, and nipping them in the bud. She says
she really cannot allow me to go so often to

the White Cottage; Mr. Cunliffe and Mr. Tudor are always there, and it is not proper. She is always hinting that I want to meet Mr. Tudor, and it is no good telling her that I never think of such a thing.' Lady Betty was half crying—a more innocent, harmless little soul never breathed; she had not a spice of coquetry in her nature. I felt indignant at such an accusation.

'It is all nonsense, Lady Betty,' I returned sharply. 'Mr. Tudor has not called at the cottage more than once since Jill left me, and then Uncle Max sent him. When I first came to Heathfield, he was very kind in doing me little services, and he dropped in two or three times when Jill was with me; but indeed he has never been a constant visitor. When we meet it is at the Vicarage, or in the street.'

'You would never convince Etta of that,' replied Lady Betty, disconsolately; 'she has even told Giles how often Mr. Tudor goes to the cottage, and she has got it into her head that I am always trying to meet him there. It is such an odious idea, only worthy of Etta herself,' went on the little girl, indignantly. 'If

I could only make her hold her tongue to Giles.'

'I would not trouble about it if I were you, dear. No one who knows you would believe it. Such an idea would never occur to Mr. Tudor; he is an honest, simple young fellow, who is not ashamed to respect women in the good old-fashioned way.'

'Oh, yes, I like him, and so does Jill; but I wish he were a thousand miles off, and then Etta would give me a little peace. How angry Gladys would be if she knew it; but I don't mean to trouble her about my small worries, poor darling.'

I had never heard Lady Betty speak with such womanly dignity. She was so often childish and whimsical that one never expected her to be grave and responsible like other people. She kissed me presently, and said I had done her good, and would I always believe in her in spite of Etta, for she was not the giddy little creature that Etta made her out to be; she was sure Giles would think more of her but for Etta's mischief-making.

Mr. Hamilton came in after this, and sat down by us, but Miss Darrell did not make her appearance until the gong sounded, and then she hurried in with a breathless apology. I do not know what made me watch her so closely all dinner-time. She took very little part in the conversation, seemed absent and thoughtful, and started nervously when Mr. Hamilton spoke to her. He told her once that she looked pale and tired, and she said then that the evening was close, and that her head ached. I wondered then if the headache had made her eyes so heavy, or if she had been crying.

Mr. Hamilton was a little quiet, too, through dinner, but listened with great interest when Lady Betty and I talked about the approaching wedding. I had to satisfy her curiosity on many points—the bride's and bridesmaids' dresses, and the programme for the day.

The details did not seem to bore Mr. Hamilton. His face never once wore its cynical expression; but when we returned to the drawing-room, and Lady Betty wanted to continue the subject, he took her quietly by the shoulders and marched her off to Miss Darrell.

'Make the child hold her tongue, Etta,' he

said good-humouredly. 'I want to coax Miss Garston to sing to us.' And then he came to me with the smile I liked best to see on his face, and held out his hand.

I was quite willing to oblige him, and he kept me hard at work for nearly an hour, first asking me if I were tired, and then begging for one more song; and sometimes I thought of Gladys as I sang, and sometimes of Max, and once of Mrs. Carrick, with her wonderful grey eyes, and false, fair face.

When I had finished I saw Mr. Hamilton looking at me rather strangely.

'Why do you sing such sad songs?' he asked in a low voice, as though he did not wish to be overheard; but he need not have been afraid—Miss Darrell was evidently taking no notice of any one just then. She was lying back in her chair with her eyes closed, and I noticed afterwards that her forehead was lined like an old woman's.

'I like melancholy songs,' was my reply, and I fingered the notes a little nervously, for his look was rather too keen just then, and I had been thinking of Mrs. Carrick.

'But you are not melancholy,' he persisted.

'There is no weak sentimentality in your nature. Just now there was a passion in your voice that startled me, as though you were drawing from some secret well.' He paused, and then went on, half playfully—

'If I were like the Hebrew steward, and asked you to let down your pitcher and give me a draught, I wonder what you would answer?'

'That would depend on circumstances. You would find it difficult to persuade me that you were thirsty, or needed anything that I could give.'

'Would it be so difficult as all that?' he returned thoughtfully. 'I thought we were better friends; that you had penetrated beneath the upper crust; that in spite of my faults you trusted me a little.'

His earnestness troubled me. I hardly knew what he meant.

'Of course we are friends,' I answered hastily. 'I can trust you more than a little.' And I would have risen from my seat, but he put his hand gently on my sleeve.

'Wait a moment. You are going away, and I may not have another opportunity. I want to tell you something. You have done me good; you have taught me that women can be trusted, after all. I thank you most heartily for that lesson.'

'I do not know what you mean,' I faltered; but I felt a singular pleasure at these words. 'I have done nothing. It is you that have been good to me.'

'Pshaw!' impatiently. 'I thought you more sensible than to say that. Now, I want you,' his voice softening again, 'to try and think better of me; not to judge by appearances, or to take other people's judgments, but to be as true and charitable to me as you are to others. Promise me this before you go, Miss Garston.'

I do not know why the tears started to my eyes. I could hardly answer him.

'Will you try to do this?' he persisted, stooping over me.

'Yes,' was my scarcely audible answer, but he was satisfied with that monosyllable. He walked away after that, and joined Lady Betty. Miss Darrell had not moved; she still lay back on the cushions, and I thought her face looked drawn and old. When I spoke to her, for it was getting late, she roused herself with difficulty.

'My head is very bad, and I shall have to go to bed, after all,' she said, giving me her hand. 'I am afraid your beautiful singing has been thrown away on me, for I was half asleep. I thought I heard you and Giles talking by the piano, but I was not sure.'

Mr. Hamilton walked home with me. He had resumed his usual manner; he told me he had had a letter that day that would oblige him to go to Edinburgh for a week or so.

'I think I shall take the night mail to-morrow evening, though it will give me a busy day; so, after all, I shall not miss you, Miss Garston.' And after a little more talk about the business that had summoned him, we reached the White Cottage, and he bade me good-bye.

'I hope you will have a pleasant holiday. Take care of yourself for all our sakes.' And with that he left me.

It was long before I slept that night. I felt confused and feverish, as though I were on the brink of some discovery that would over-whelm and alarm me. I could not understand myself or Mr. Hamilton. His words presented an enigma. I felt troubled by them, and yet not unhappy.

Had Miss Darrell overheard him, I wondered. I felt, if she had done so, her manner would have been different. She seemed jealous of her cousin, and always monopolised his words and looks. He had never spoken to me a dozen words in her presence that she had not tried to interrupt us. Had she really been asleep? These doubts kept recurring to me. Just before I fell asleep a remembrance of Leah's sullen face came between me and my dreams. Her insolent voice rang in my ears. What had she meant by her words? Why had Miss Darrell submitted to her impertinence? Was she afraid of Leah, as Gladys said? I began to feel weary of all these mysteries.

T

CHAPTER XXX.

WITH TIMBRELS AND DANCES.

UNT Philippa and Sara came to meet me at Victoria. They both seemed unfeignedly glad to see me.

Aunt Philippa was certainly a kind-hearted woman. Her faults were those that were engendered by too much prosperity. Overmuch ease and luxury had made her lymphatic and indolent. Except for Ralph's death she had never known sorrow. Care had not yet traced a single line on her smooth forehead; it looked as open and unfurrowed as a child's. Contentment, a comfortable self-complacency, were written on her comely face. Just now it beamed with motherly welcome. Somehow, I never felt so fond of Aunt Philippa as I did at that moment when she leant over the carriage with outstretched hands to kiss me.

'My dear, how well you are looking. Five years younger. Does she not look well, Sara?'

Sara nodded and smiled, and made room for me to pass her, and then gave orders that my luggage should be entrusted to the maid, who would convey it in a cab to Hyde Park Gate.

'If you do not mind, Ursula, we are going round the Park for a little,' observed Sara, with a pretty blush.

Her mother laughed. 'Colonel Ferguson is riding in the Row, and will be looking out for us. He is coming this evening, as usual, but Sara thinks four-and-twenty hours too long to wait.'

'Oh, mother, how can you talk so!' returned Sara, bashfully. 'You know Donald asked us to meet him, and he would be so disappointed. And it is such a lovely afternoon—if Ursula does not mind.'

'On the contrary I shall like it very much,' I returned, moved by curiosity to see Colonel Ferguson again. I had never seen him by daylight, and though we had often met at the evening receptions we had not exchanged a dozen words.

I thought Sara was looking prettier than ever. A sort of radiance seemed to surround her. Youth and beauty, perfect health, a light heart, and satisfied affections; these were the gifts of the gods that had been showered upon her. Would those bright smiling eyes ever shed tears, I wondered. Would any sorrow drive away that light careless gaiety? I hoped not. It was pleasant to see any one so happy. And then I thought of Lesbia and Gladys, and sighed.

'You do not look at all tired, Ursie,' observed Sara, affectionately, laying her little gloved hand on mine. 'She looks quite nice and fresh—does she not, mother? I was so afraid that you would have come up in your nurse's livery, as Jocelyn calls it—black serge, and a horrid dowdy bonnet.'

'Oh no! I knew better than that,' I returned, with a complacent glance at my handsome black silk, one of Uncle Brian's presents. I had the comfortable conviction that even Sara could not find fault with my bonnet and mantle. I had made a careful toilette purposely, for I knew what importance they attached to such things. Sara's little speech rewarded me, as well as Aunt Philippa's approving look.

'It has not done her any harm,' I heard her observe *sotto voce*. 'She certainly looks younger.'

I took advantage of a pause in Sara's chatter to ask after Jill. Aunt Philippa answered me, for Sara was bowing towards a passing carriage.

'Oh, poor child, she wanted to come with us to meet you, but it was Professor Hugel's afternoon. He teaches her German literature, you know. I was anxious for her not to miss his lesson, and she was very good about it. She is coming down to afternoon tea, and of course we shall see her in the evening.'

'Poor dear Jocelyn; she was longing to come, I know. You and Miss Gillespie are terribly severe,' observed Sara, with a light laugh. She was so free and gay herself, that she rather pitied her young sister, condemned to the daily grind of lessons and hard work.

'Nonsense, Sara,' returned her mother, sharply. 'We are not severe at all. Jocelyn knows that it is all for her good if Miss Gillespie keeps her to her task. My dear Ursula, we are all charmed with Miss Gillespie—even Sara, though she pretends to call her strict and old-fashioned. She is a most amiable, ladylike woman, and Jocelyn is perfectly happy with her.'

'I am very pleased with Jocelyn,' she went on. 'You have done her good, Ursula, and both her father and I are very grateful to you. She is not nearly so wayward and self-willed. She takes great pains with her lessons, and is most industrious. She is not so awkward, either, and Miss Gillespie thinks it will be a good plan if I take her out with me driving sometimes when Sara is married. I shall only have Jocelyn then,' finished Aunt Philippa, with a regretful look at her daughter. I was much interested in all they had to tell me, but I was not sorry when we entered the Park and the stream of talk died away.

I almost felt as though I were in a dream, as the moving kaleidoscope of horses and carriages and foot passengers passed before my eyes.

Yesterday, at this time, I was sitting in poor Robert Lambert's whitewashed attic, listening to the sparrows that were twittering under the eaves. When I had left the cottage I had walked down country roads, meeting nothing but a donkey-cart and two tramps.

Now, the sunshine was playing on the rhododendrons and on the green leaves of the trees in Hyde Park. A brass band had struck up in the distance. The riders were cantering up and down the Row, to the admiration of the well-dressed crowds that sauntered under the trees or lingered by the railings. Carriages were passing and repassing. A four-in-hand drove past us, followed by a tandem. Beautiful young faces smiled out of the carriages. A few of them looked weary and care-worn. Now and then, under the smart bonnet, one saw the pinched weazened face of old age—dowagers in big fur capes looking out with their dim hungry eyes on the follies of Vanity Fair. One wondered at the set senile smile on these old faces; they had fed on husks all their lives, and the food had failed to nourish them ; their strength had failed over the battle of life, but they still refused to leave the field of their former triumphs. Everywhere in these fashionable crowds one sees these pale meagre faces that belong to a past age. They wear gorgeous velvets, jewels, feathers, paint—like Jezebel, they would look out of the window curiously to the last. How one longs to take them gently out of the crowd, to wash their poor cheeks, and lead them to some quiet home, where they may shut their tired eyes in peace. 'What is the world to you?' one would say to them. 'You have done all your tasks, well or badly; leave the arena to the young and the strong, it is no place for you; come home and rest, before the Dark Angel finds you in your tinsel and gew-gaws.' Would they listen to me, I wonder?

Sara's soft dimples came into play presently. A pretty blush rose to her face. A tall man with a bronzed handsome face and iron grey moustache had detached himself from the other riders, and was cantering towards the carriage that was now drawn up near the entrance; in another moment he had checked his horse with some difficulty.

'I have been looking out for you the last three-quarters of an hour,' he said, addressing Sara. 'I could not see the carriage anywhere. Miss Garston, we have met before, but I think we hardly know each other,' looking at me with some degree of interest. Sara's cousin was no longer indifferent to him.

I answered him as civilly as I could, but I could see his attention wandered to his young *fiancée*, and he soon rode round to her side of the carriage. It was evident, as Lesbia said, that the Colonel was honestly in love with Sara. She looked very young beside him, but there must have been something very winning in her sweet looks and words to the man who had known trouble, and had laid a young wife and child to rest in an Indian grave.

Before the evening was over I felt I liked Colonel Ferguson immensely, and thought far more of Sara for being his choice; there was an air of frankness and *bonhomie* about him, that won one's heart; he was sensible and practical. In spite of his fondness for Sara, he would keep her in order—one could see that. I heard him rebuke her very gently that first evening for some extravagance she was planning. They were standing apart from the others on the balcony, but I was near the open window, and I heard him say distinctly in a grave voice,

'I am very sorry to disappoint you, but I

must ask you to give up this idea, my darling; it would not be right in our position; surely you must see that.'

'No, Donald, I do not see it a bit,' she answered quickly.

'Then will you be satisfied with my seeing it, and give it up for my sake, dear?'

I knew when they came back into the room that he had got his way. Sara was smiling as happily as usual; her disappointment had not gone very deep; her future husband would have very little trouble with her. She was neither self-willed nor selfish. She wanted to be happy herself and make other people happy; she would be easily guided.

When we left the Park Colonel Ferguson rode off to his club, and we drove home rather quickly. There were some visitors waiting for Sara in the drawing-room, so I went up to my old room to take off my bonnet. Martha would unpack my boxes, Aunt Philippa told me, as she gave me another kiss in the hall.

I had not been there for five minutes when I heard flying footsteps down the passage, and the next moment Jill's strong arms had taken me by the shoulders and turned me round.

'Now, Jill, I don't mean to be strangled as usual;' but she left me no breath for more.

'Oh, my dear precious old Bear, this is too good to be true. I nearly cried with joy this morning, at the idea of seeing you in your old room, and knowing you will be here a whole fortnight. I declare, after all, Sara is very nice to get married.'

No, Jill was not changed; she was as real and big and demonstrative as usual; but somehow she looked nicer.

'You must be quick,' she continued, 'for father has come in, and Clayton has taken in the tea. We must go down directly; but I want you to see Miss Gillespie first,' and Jill looked proud and eager as she led me down the passage.

The schoolroom was still the same dull back room that Aunt Philippa thought so conducive to her young daughter's studies, but it certainly looked more cheerful this evening.

The window was opened, there was a window-box full of gay flowers. A great bowl of my favourite wall-flowers was on the table, another vase with trails of laburnum and lilac was on Jill's little table. The fresh air and sunshine and the sweet scent of the flowers had quite transformed the dingy room; there was new cretonne on the old sofa, a handsome cloth on the centre table, a new easy-chair.

Miss Gillespie was sitting by the window reading. She had an interesting face and rather sad grey eyes; but her manner was decidedly prepossessing.

She looked at her pupil with affection. Evidently Jill's abruptness and awkwardness were not misunderstood by her.

'I want you two to like each other,' Jill had said, without a pretence of introduction; and we had both laughed and extended our hands.

'I seem to know you already, Miss Garston,' she said in a pleasant voice. 'Jocelyn talks about you so much, that you cannot be a stranger to me. Do you know your father has come in, dear?' turning to Jill.

'Yes, and I must take my cousin downstairs. Good-bye for the present, Gypsy.'

Miss Gillespie smiled again when she saw my astonishment at Jill's familiarity.

'Jocelyn thinks my name too long, and has abbreviated it to Gypsy. Mrs. Garston was terribly shocked at first, but I told her that it did not matter in the least; in fact, I like it.'

'She is such a dear old thing,' burst out Jill, as we left the schoolroom and proceeded downstairs arm in arm. 'I never think of her as my governess; she is just a kind friend who helps me with my lessons and walks with me. We do have such cosy times together. Does not the schoolroom look nice, Ursie?'

'Very nice, indeed, my dear.'

'So I think; but Sara says it is horrid; she has made mother promise to give me her room directly she is married. Sara has a beautiful piano there, and a bookcase, and all sorts of pretty things. It is a lovely room, you know, and looks out over the Park. Mother thinks it too nice and pretty for a schoolroom; but I am to call it my study, and keep it tidy. And Gypsy is to have the old schoolroom for herself, so we are both pleased. It is nice for her to have a room of her own, where she can be alone.'

' Your mother is very kind to you, Jill.'

' Awfully kind—I mean very kind—Gypsy does so dislike that expression. Do you know, I think you two are rather alike in that? Gypsy is very unhappy sometimes, though. I have found her crying more than once when I have left her long alone; only mother does not know, and I don't mean to tell her, because she thinks people ought always to be cheerful. It was so sad that clergyman dying—the one she was to marry; his name was Maurice Compton. I saw the name in one of her books—" Lilian Gillespie, from her devoted friend, Maurice Compton."'

' My dear Jill, how long are you going to keep me standing in the hall? Clayton will find us here directly.'

' Yes, I know;' but Jill showed no intention of moving—the prospect of cold tea did not trouble her; ' but I want to tell you something before you go in. Mother is certainly kinder to me than she ever has been; she says I am to drive with her very often, and that she shall take me to see picture galleries. And father is going to buy a horse for me, because he says I ride so well that I may go out

with him as a rule instead of with a master;
and—'

'You shall tell me all that presently,' I
returned, 'for I am too tired to stand on this
mat any longer. Are you coming, Jill, or shall
I go in without you?' but of course I knew
she would follow me.

The room seemed full when we entered.
Aunt Philippa was at the tea-table, Sara flitting
about the room from one guest to another.
Uncle Brian, who was standing on the hearth-
rug, put out his hand to me.

' I am glad to see you back again, Ursula,'
looking at me with his cool, penetrating glance.
Uncle Brian was never demonstrative. ' I
think the work suits you, to judge by your
looks; take that chair by your aunt, child, and
she will give you some tea.' And accordingly
I placed myself under Aunt Philippa's wing,
while Jill and a boy officer with a budding
moustache waited on me.

The rest of the evening passed very pleasantly. I had a long conversation with Miss
Gillespie in the inner drawing-room, while
Sara and Jill played duets; of course our
subject was Jill. Miss Gillespie spoke most

warmly of her excellent abilities, and fine development of character. 'She will be a very striking woman,' she finished, when the last chords were played, and a soft clapping of hands succeeded. 'Whether she will be a happy one is more doubtful; she must not be thwarted too much, and she must have room to expand. Jocelyn wants space and sunshine.'

I thought these remarks very sensible; they taught me that Miss Gillespie had grasped the true idea of Jill's character; there was nothing little about Jill—she never did things by halves; she either loved or hated; she was truthful to a fault. There was a massive freedom and simplicity about her that would guide her safely through the world's pitfalls. 'Space and sunshine,' that was all Jill needed to bring her to maturity and fruition. Some girls may be trusted to educate themselves. Jill was one of these.

The next morning Sara took possession of me. A great honour was to be vouchsafed me. I was to be treated to a private view of the trousseau and wedding presents.

I had exhausted my vocabulary of admiring epithets, and sat in eloquent silence long before Sara had finished her display. It was like the picture of Pandora opening her box, to see the pretty creature opening the big, carved wardrobe to show me the layers of delicate, embroidered raiment, muslin and laces and jewels, curious trinkets and wonderful gifts worthy of the Arabian Nights. There were two rooms full of treasures that had been laid at her feet, and no doubt, like Pandora, Sara had the rainbow-tinted hope lying amid the bridal gifts.

'This is Donald's present,' she said, smiling, showing me a diamond spray. 'I am to wear it on Thursday; it is the loveliest present of all—though mother has given me that beautiful pearl necklace.'

'Wait a moment, Sara,' I said, detaining her as she closed the morocco case; 'tell me, do you not feel like a princess in Fairyland, with all this glitter round you? Does it all seem real somehow?'

'Donald is real, anyhow,' she returned, with a charming blush. 'Nothing would be real without him. Oh, Ursula, it is nice to be so happy. I always have been happier than other girls,' and something like a tear stole to her pretty eyes.

'Now you must see your own dress,' she continued, brushing off the tiny tear-drop, with a laugh at her own sentimentality, 'What do you think of that; is that not charming taste?'

'It is far too good for me,' I returned seriously. 'How could Uncle Brian buy that for me?—it is beautiful, it is perfect, and just my taste.' And then I could say no more, for Sara had placed her hands across my lips to silence me.

'Then you must wear it, dear. Father and mother wanted to give you something nice, because you were so good to Jocelyn, and I knew you had a fancy for a velvet gown: is not that yellowish lace charming, Ursula, and the bonnet harmonises so well? Your bouquet is to be cream-coloured too, with just a tea-rose or so. You will look quite pretty in it, Ursula dear. Do you know Donald liked the look of you so yesterday—he said you looked so strong and sensible; he called you an interesting woman.'

I hastened to change the subject, for it recalled certain words that I vainly tried to forget. It was a relief when visitors were announced, and Sara left me to go down to the drawing-room. I was glad to be alone for a few minutes. Aunt Philippa came up soon afterwards with a bevy of friends, and I escaped to my own room until luncheon-time.

I grew a little weary of the bustle by-and-by, and yet I was pleased and interested too ; the excitement was infectious—one smiled to see so many happy faces ; and then there was so much to do, every one was pressed into the service. Jill shut up her books with a bang, her piano remained closed. She and Miss Gillespie were answering notes, unpacking presents, running to and fro with messages ; people came all day long—they talked in corners on the balcony, in Uncle Brian's study ; no room was held sacred.

A cargo of flowers arrived presently ; the hall and drawing-room were to be transformed into bowers. It must rain roses as well as sunshine on the young princess. Sara's bright face appeared every now and then among the workers ; a little court surrounded her—sometimes Colonel Ferguson's bronzed face looked over her shoulders.

'That is very pretty, Ursula. I see you have caught the right idea. Jocelyn dear, you are overfilling that basket. and some of the stalks are showing. Miss Gillespie will put it right for you. Come, Grace, shall we go up-stairs?'

Sara nodded and smiled at us as she led the way to the upper regions. Pandora was for ever opening her box in those days—she was never weary of fingering her silks and satins.

'Now she has gone. let us rest a little,' Jill exclaimed, letting her arms fall to her side. 'Are you not tired of it all, Ursie dear? I get so giddy that I keep rubbing my eyes. I never knew weddings meant all this fuss. Why cannot people do things more quietly? If I ever get married I shall just put on my bonnet and walk to the nearest church with father. What is the use of all this nonsense? It is like decking the victim for the sacrifice, to see all these roses and green leaves. Supposing we have a band of music to drown her groans while she is dressing,' finished Jill, re-belliously, as she contemplated her flower-basket with dissatisfied eyes.

Jill's speech recalled Mr. Hamilton's words most vividly. 'Because two people elect to join hands for the journey of life, is there any adequate reason why all their idle acquaintances should accompany them with cymbals and prancings, and all sorts of fooleries, just at the most solemn moment of life?' and again, "Till death us do part"—can any one, man or woman, say those words lightly and not bring down a doom upon himself?'

Could I ever forget how solemnly he had said this? After all, Mr. Hamilton was right, and I think Jill was right too.

CHAPTER XXXI.

WEDDING CHIMES.

WHEN we had finished the flowers and brought in Aunt Philippa to see the effect, I left the others and went up to my room. I had been busy since the early morning and felt I had fairly earned a little rest.

The room that was still called mine had a side window looking over the Park. Down below carriages were passing and repassing, a detachment of Hussars trotted past, people were pouring out from the Albert Hall—some afternoon concert was just over; the children were playing as usual on the grass; the soft evening shadows were creeping up between the trees, the sky was blue and cloudless. May was

wearing her choicest smiles on the eve of
Sara's wedding-day.

Martha, the schoolroom maid, had brought
me a cup of tea; the rest of the family were
crowded in Uncle Brian's study, the dining-
room was already in the hands of Gunter's
assistants; the long drawing-room and inner
drawing-room were sweet with roses and
baskets of costly hot-house flowers; a bank of
rhododendrons was under the hall window; the
house was full of sunshine, flowers, and the
ripple of laughter. I could hear the laughter
through the closed door, Sara's musical tinkle
rang out whenever the door opened. I had
fallen into a sort of waking dream, when something white and golden passed between me and
the sunlight; a light kiss was dropped on my
drowsy eyelids, and there was Lesbia smiling
at me.

She looked so cool and fair in her white
gown, with a tiny bouquet of delicious tea-roses
in her hand, her golden hair shining under her
little lace bonnet. I thought she looked more
than ever like Charlie's white lily, only now
there was a touch of colour on her face.

'Oh, Ursie dear, I am so pleased to see

you,' she said gently, laying the flowers on my lap. 'Clayton told me that every one else was in Mr. Garston's study, so I begged to run up here. We only came up from Rutherford this morning, and we have been so busy ever since. I was afraid you were asleep, for I knocked at the door without getting any answer; but no, your eyes were wide open, so you were only dreaming.'

'I believe I was very tired, they have kept me running about all day; take this low chair by the window, dear, and tell me all about yourself. Do you know it is six months since we met, there must be so much to say on both sides; but first, how is Mrs. Fullertor, and is it Rutherford that has given you those pretty roses, Lesbia?' But the roses I meant were certainly not on my lap.

She answered literally and seriously in her usual way. 'Yes, they are from Rutherford; I cut them myself in spite of Patrick's grumbling. Mother is very well, Ursula; I am sure the country agrees with her. We have been there since March, and these two months have been the happiest to me since dear Charlie died.'

'You need not tell me that,' I returned,

with a satisfied look at the sweet face. ' Health
has returned to you, you are no longer languid
and weary; your eyes are bright, your voice
has a stronger tone in it.'

' Is it wrong,' she answered quickly? ' I do
not forget, I shall never forget, but the pain
seems soothed somehow.   When I wake up
in the bed where I slept as a child I hear the
birds singing, and I do not say to myself,
'' Here is another long weary day to get
through."   On the contrary, I jump up and
dress myself as quickly as I can, for I love
to be out among the dews; everything is so
sweet and still in the early morning—there is
such freshness in the air.'

' And these early walks are good for you.'

' Oh, I never leave the grounds, I just
saunter about with Flo and Rover; when
breakfast is ready I have a bouquet to lay
beside mother's plate. Dear, good mother—do
you know she cannot say enough in praise of
Rutherford, now she sees the breakfasts I eat? I
think she would be reconciled to any place if
she saw me enjoy my food; at the Albert Hall
Mansions I never felt hungry, I was always too
tired to eat.'

'I knew Mrs. Fullerton would never repent her sacrifice.'

'No, indeed; mother and I have never been so cosy in our lives. She sits in the veranda and laughs over my quarrels with Patrick; he is quite as crossgrained as ever, dear old fellow, but there is nothing that he will not do for me. We are making a rose-garden now. Do you remember that sunny corner by the terrace and sun-dial?—dear Charlie always wanted me to have a rose-garden there; we have trellis-work arches and a little arbour. Patrick and Hawkins are doing the work, but I fancy they cannot get on without me.'

She stopped with a little laugh at her own conceit, and then went on—

'And I am so busy in other ways, Ursula. Every Monday I go to the mothers' meeting with Mrs. Trevor, and I have some of the old women at the almshouses beside—I am so fond of those old women—and I have just begun afternoons for tennis; people like these, and they come from such a distance. Mr. Manners declares the Rutherford Thursdays will soon be known all over the country.'

'Bravo, Lesbia, you are taking your position nobly, my dear; this is just what Charlie wanted to see you, a brave sweet woman who would not let sorrow and disappointment spoil her own and other people's lives.' Then as she blushed with pleasure at my words, I said carelessly, 'Do you often see Mr. Manners?'

'Oh, yes,' she returned without hesitation, 'on my Thursdays and at church, and at the Vicarage—we are always meeting somewhere. He was Charlie's friend, you know, and he is so nice and sympathising, and tells me so much about their school life and college life together; he was so fond of Charlie, and the undergraduates used to call them Damon and Pythias.'

'To be sure, Charlie was always talking about Harcourt. He has grown very handsome, I have heard.'

'Mother says so; he is certainly good-looking,' she answered simply; 'and then he is so kind. I feel almost ashamed at troubling him so much with our business and commissions, but he never seems to mind any amount of trouble. I have never met any one so unselfish.'

I turned away my head to hide a smile. Lesbia was quite serious. She was too much absorbed in the memory of Charlie to read the secret of Harcourt Manners' unselfishness; the kindly attentions of the young man, his solicitude and sympathy, have not yet awakened a suspicion of the truth.

One day Lesbia's eyes would be opened, and she would be shocked and surprised to find the hold that Charlie's friend had got over her heart. Very likely she would dismiss him and lock herself up in her room and cry for hours; probably she would persist for some weeks in making herself and him exceedingly unhappy. But it would be all no use; the tie of sympathy would be too strong; he would have made himself too necessary to her. One day she would have to yield, and find her life's happiness in thus yielding. Charlie's white lily was too fair to be left to wither alone, and I knew Harcourt Manners would be worthy to win the prize.

I could see it all before it happened, while Lesbia talked in her serious way of Mr. Manners' unselfishness. Presently, however, she changed the subject, and began questioning me eagerly about my work; and just then Jill joined us, and placed herself on the floor at my feet, with the firm intention evidently of listening to our remarks.

The conversation drifted round to Gladwyn presently. I could see Lesbia was a little curious about these friends of mine that I had mentioned casually in my letters.

'I can't quite make out the relationship,' she said in a puzzled tone ; 'you are always talking about this Gladys. Is she really so beautiful and fascinating? And who is Miss Darrell ? '

'You had better ask me,' interrupted Jill quite rudely, 'for Ursula is so absurdly infatuated about the whole family ; she thinks them all quite perfect, with the exception of the double-faced lady, Miss Darrell ; but they are very ordinary, quite ordinary people, I assure you.'

'Now, Jill, we do not want any of your impertinence. Lesbia would rather hear my description of my friends.'

'On the contrary, she would prefer the opinion of an unprejudiced person,' persisted Jill, with a voluble eloquence that took away my breath. 'Listen to me, Lesbia. This Mr. Hamilton that Ursula is always talking about '—

how I longed to box Jill's pretty little ears; she had lovely ears, pink and shell-like, hidden under her black locks—' is an ugly, disagreeable-looking man.'

'Oh !' from Lesbia, in rather a disappointed tone.

' He is quite old, about five-and-thirty they say, and he has a long smooth-shaven face like a Jesuit. I don't recollect seeing a Jesuit though, but he is very like one all the same. He has dark eyes that stare somehow and seem to put you down, and he has a way of laughing at you civilly that makes you wild; and Ursula believes in him, and is quite meek in his presence—just because he is a doctor and orders her about.'

' My dear Lesbia, I hope you are taking Jill's measure with a grain of salt. Mr. Hamilton is not disagreeable, and he never orders me about.'

Jill shook her head at me, and went on—

' Then there is the double-faced lady—but never mind her; we both hate her.'

' You mean Miss Darrell, Mr. Hamilton's cousin ? '

' Yes, Witch-Etta, as Lady Betty calls her.

She is a dark-eyed, slim piece of elegance, utterly dependent on her clothes for beauty; she dresses perfectly, and makes herself out a good-looking woman, but she is not really good-looking; and she is always talking, and her talk is exciting, because there is always something behind her words, something mildly suggestive of volcanoes, or something equally pleasant and enlivening. If she smiles, for instance, one seems to think one must find out the meaning of that.'

'Who has taught you all this, Jill?' asked Lesbia, bewildered by this sarcasm.

'My mother-wit,' returned Jill, utterly un-abashed. 'Well, then there is Gladys. Ah, now we are coming to the saddest part. Once upon a time there was a beautiful maiden, really a lovely creature—oh, I grant you that, Ursula—but she fell under the power of some wicked magician, male or female—some folks say Witch-Etta—who changed her into a snow-maiden or an ice-maiden. If she were only alive, this Gladys would be most lovely and bewitching, but you see she is only a poor snow-maiden, very white and cold. If she gives you her hand, it quite freezes you; her kiss turns you to ice too; her smile is congealing. Ursula tries to thaw her sometimes, but it does no good. She is only Gladys, the snow-maiden.'

I was too angry with Jill to say a word. Lesbia looked more mystified than ever.

'If she be so cold and sad, how can Ursula be so fond of her?' she demanded in her practical way. But Jill took no notice, but rattled on—

'Little brown Betsy—I beg her pardon— Lady Betty is the best of all, she is really human. Gladys is only half alive. Lady Betty laughs and talks and pouts; she wrinkles up like an old woman when she is cross, and has lovely dimples when she smiles. She is not pretty, but she is quaint, and interesting, and child-like. I am very fond of Lady Betty,' finished Jill, with a benevolent nod.

I proceeded to annotate Jill's mischievous remarks with much severity. I left Mr. Hamilton alone, with the exception of a brief sentence; I assured Lesbia that he was not ugly, but only peculiar-looking, and that he was an intellectual, earnest-minded man, who had known much trouble. Jill made a wry face, but did not dare to contradict me.

'As for his sister Gladys,' I went on, 'she was simply a most beautiful girl, whose health had failed a little from a great shock;' here Jill and Lesbia both looked curious, but I showed no intention of enlightening them. 'She is a little too sad and quiet for Jill's taste,' I continued, 'and she is also somewhat reserved in manner, but when she likes a person thoroughly she is charming.'

I went on a little more in this strain, until I had thoroughly vindicated my favourite from Jill's aspersion.

'You are very fond of her, Ursula; your eyes soften as you talk of her. I should like to see this wonderful Gladys.'

'You must see her one day,' I rejoined; and then the gong sounded, and Lesbia jumped up in a fright, because she said she would keep her mother waiting, and Jill hurried off to her room to dress.

We had what Jill called a picnic dinner in Uncle Brian's study. Every one enjoyed it but Clayton, who seemed rather put out by the disorganised state of the house, and who was always getting helplessly wedged in between the escritoire and the table. We would have much rather waited on ourselves, and we wished Mrs. Martin had foregone the usual number of courses. When it was over we all went into the long drawing-room, and Jill played soft snatches of Chopin, while Sara and Colonel Ferguson whispered together on the dark balcony.

Mrs. Fullerton and Lesbia joined us later on, and then Colonel Ferguson took his leave. I thought Sara looked a little quiet and subdued when she joined us; her gay chatter had died away, her eyes were a little plaintive. When we had said good-night, and Jill and I were passing down the corridor hand in hand, we could hear voices from Aunt Philippa's room. Through the half opened door I caught a glimpse of Sara; she was kneeling by her mother's chair, with her head on Aunt Philippa's shoulder. Was she bidding a tearful regret to her old happy life, I wondered—was she looking forward with natural shrinking and a little fear to the new responsiblity that awaited her on the morrow? It was the mother who was talking; one could imagine how her heart would yearn over her child to-night—what fond prayers would be uttered for the girl.

Aunt Philippa was a loving mother, worldliness had not touched the ingrained warmth of her nature.

I am glad to remember how brightly the sun shone on Sara's wedding-day—there was not a cloud in the sky. When I woke the birds were singing in Hyde Park, and Jill in her white wrapper was looking at me with bright, excited eyes.

'It is such a lovely morning!' she exclaimed rapturously. 'Actually Sara is asleep, fancy sleeping under such circumstances! She and mother are going to have breakfast together in the schoolroom—do be quick and dress, Ursula; father is always so early, you know.'

Uncle Brian was reading his paper as usual when I entered the study. Miss Gillespie was pouring out coffee. Jill was fidgeting about the room, until her father called her to order, and then she sat down to the table. I do not think any of us enjoyed our breakfast. Uncle Brian certainly looked dull, Jill was too excited to eat, poor Miss Gillespie had tears in her eyes; she poured out tea and coffee with cold shaking hands. 'Lilian Gillespie, from her devoted friend Maurice Compton,' came into my head; no wonder the thought of marriage bells and bridal finery made her sad. I am afraid I should have shut myself up in my own room, and refused to mingle with the crowd under these circumstances. I quite understood the feeling of sympathy that made Jill stoop down and kiss the smooth brown hair as she passed the governess's chair—it was a sort of affectionate homage to misfortune patiently borne.

I went up to the schoolroom when breakfast was over. Aunt Philippa looked as though she had not slept—there was a jaded look about her eyes. Sara, on the contrary, looked fresh and smiling; she was just going to put herself in her maid's hands; but she tripped back in her pretty muslin dressing-gown and rose-coloured ribbons to kiss me and ask me to look after Jill's toilette.

'Every one is so busy, and mother and Draper will be attending to me—do please, Ursie dear, see that she puts on her bonnet straight.' And of course I promised to do my best.

As it happened, Jill was very tractable and

obedient. I think her beautiful bridesmaid's dress rather impressed her. I saw a look of awe in her eyes as she regarded herself, and then she dropped a mocking curtsy to her own image.

'I am Jocelyn to-day, remember that, Ursula. I don't look a bit like Jill—Jocelyn Adelaide Garston, bridesmaid.'

'You look charming, Jill — I mean Jocelyn.'

'Oh, how horrid it sounds from your lips, Ursie. I like my own funny little name best from you; now come and let me finish you.' And Jill, in spite of her fine dress, would persist in waiting on me. She was very voluble in her expression of admiration when I had finished, but I did not seem to recognise 'Nurse Ursula' in the elegantly-dressed woman that I saw reflected in the pier-glass. 'Fine feathers make fine birds,' I said to myself.

I think we all agreed that Sara looked lovely. Lesbia, who joined us in the drawing-room, contemplated her with tears in her eyes.

'You look like a picture, Sara,' she whispered, 'like a fairy queen, in all that white-ness.' Sara dimpled and blushed. Of course she knew how pretty she was, and how people liked to look at her; but I am sure she was thinking of Donald, as her eyes rested on her bridal bouquet. Dearly as she loved all this finery and consequence, there was a soft, thoughtful expression in her eyes that was quite new to them, and that I loved to see.

We went to church presently, and Lesbia and I, standing side by side, heard the beautiful awful service—'till death us do part.' Oh, what words to say to any man! Surely false lips would grow paralysed over them!

A most curious thing happened just then. I had raised my eyes, when they suddenly encountered Mr. Hamilton's. A sort of shock crossed me. Why was he here? How had he come? How strange, how very strange! The next moment he had disappeared from my view; probably he had withdrawn behind a pillar that he might not attract my notice. I could almost have believed that it was an illusion and fancied resemblance, only I had never seen a face like Mr. Hamilton's.

The momentary glimpse had distracted me, and I heard the remainder of the service rather absently; then the pealing notes of the wedding march resounded through the church; we all stood waiting until Sara had signed her name, and had come out of the vestry leaning on her husband's arm.

I was under Major Egerton's care. The crowd round the door was so great that it was with the greatest difficulty that he could pilot me to the carriage. Lesbia was following us with another officer, whose name I did not know. As we took our seats I saw Mr. Hamilton distinctly cross the road. He was walking quietly down Hyde Park. As we passed he turned and took off his hat. I thought it was a strange thing that he should be in the neighbourhood on Sara's wedding-day, and that he should have deigned to play the part of a spectator after his severe strictures on gay weddings. I supposed his business in Edinburgh was finished, and he had an idle day or two on his hands. I half expected him to call the next day, for I had given him my address; but he did not come, and I heard from Mr. Tudor afterwards that he had gone on to Folkestone.

CHAPTER XXXII.

A FIERY ORDEAL.

IT is a hackneyed truism, and, like other axioms, profoundly true, that wedding festivities are invariably followed by a sense of blank dulness.

It is like the early morning after a ball, when the last guests have left the house,—the lights flicker in the dawn, the empty rooms want sweeping and furnishing to be fit for habitation. Yawns, weariness, satiety, drive the jaded entertainers to their resting-places. Every one knows how tawdry the ball-dress looks in the clear morning light. The diamonds cease to flash, the flowers are withered, the game is played out.

Something of this languor and vacuum are felt when the bride and bridegroom have driven away amid the typical shower of rice

The smiles seem quenched somehow; mother and sisters shed tears; a sense of loss pervades the house; the bridal finery is heaped up in the empty room; one little glove is on the table, another has fallen to the floor. All sorts of girlish trinkets that have been forgotten lie unheeded in corners.

I know we all thought that evening would never end, and I quite understood why Jill hovered near her mother's chair, listening to her conversation with Mrs. Fullerton. Every now and then Aunt Philippa broke down and shed a few quiet tears. I heard her mention Ralph's name once. 'Poor boy, how proud he would have been of his sister!' Uncle Brian heard it, too, for I saw him wince at the sound of his son's name; but Jill stroked her mother's hand, and said quite naturally, 'Most likely Ralph knows all about it, mamma, and of course he is glad that Sara is so happy.'

Our pretty light-hearted Sara. I had no idea that I should miss her so much! Indeed we all missed her; it seemed to me now that I had undervalued her. True, she had not been a congenial companion to me in my dark days; but even then I had wronged her. Why should I have expected her to grope among the shadows with me, instead of following her into the sunshine? Sara could not act contrary to her nature: sad things depressed her. She wanted to cause every one to be happy.

Her feelings were far deeper than I had imagined them to be. I liked the way she spoke to Jill when she was bidding good-bye to us all.

'Jocelyn, dear, promise me that you will be good to mother. She has no one but you now to study her little ways and make her comfortable, and she is not as young as she was, and things tire her.' Of course Jill promised with tears in her eyes, and Sara went away smiling and radiant. Jill was already trying to redeem her promise, as she hovered like a tall slim shadow behind her mother's chair in the twilight.

'Come and sit down, Jocelyn, my dear,' observed Aunt Philippa at last, in her motherly voice. When I looked again Jill's black locks were bobbing on her mother's lap, and the three seemed all talking together.

There was very little rest for any one during the next few days. Sara's marriage had brought sundry relations from their country homes up to

town, and there was open house kept for all.
Jill went sight-seeing with the young people.
Aunt Philippa drove some of the elder ladies
to the Academy, to the Grosvenor Gallery, to
the Park, and other places.

Every day there were luncheon parties, tea
parties, dinner parties; the long drawing-room
seemed full every evening. Jill put on one or
other of her pretty new gowns, and played her
pieces industriously; there was no stealing away
in corners now. There were round games for the
young people; now and then they went to the
theatre or opera—no wonder Jill was too tired
and excited to open her lesson-books. My
fortnight's visit extended itself to three weeks.
Aunt Philippa could not spare me; she said I
was much too useful to her and Uncle Brian.
I wrote to Mrs. Barton and also to Lady Betty.
and I begged the latter to inform her brother
that I could not leave my relations just yet.

Lady Betty wrote back at once. She had
given my message, she said, but Giles had not
seemed half pleased with it. She thought he
was going away somewhere. she did not know
where; but he had told her to say that there
were no fresh cases, and that Robert Lambert

was going on all right, and that as I seemed enjoying myself so much it was a pity not to take a longer holiday while I was about it, and he sent his kind regards—and that was all. I suppose I ought to have been satisfied, but it struck me that there was a flavour of sarcasm about Mr. Hamilton's message.

But he was right—I was enjoying myself. Lesbia was still in town, and I saw her every day; my acquaintance with Miss Gillespie grew to intimacy, and I think we mutually enjoyed each other's society. Aunt Philippa seemed to turn to me naturally for help and comfort, and her constant 'Ursula, my dear, will you do this for me?' gave me a real feeling of pleasure; and then there was Jill to pet and praise at every odd moment.

One day we were all called upon to admire Sara's new signature, 'Sara Ferguson,' written in bold girlish characters. 'Donald is looking over my shoulder as I write it, dear mamma,' Sara wrote in a long postscript: 'are husbands always so impertinent? Donald pretends that it is part of his duty to see that I dot my i's and cross my t's; he will talk such nonsense. There, he has gone off laughing, and I

may end comfortably by telling you that he
spoils me dreadfully and is so good to me, and
that I am happier than I deserve to be, and
your very loving child, Sara.'

'Poor darling, she always did make her
own sunshine,' murmured Aunt Philippa, fondly.

Now, that afternoon who should call upon·
us but Mr. Tudor. Jill was out as usual riding
with two of her cousins and Uncle Brian. They
had gone off to Kew or Richmond for the afternoon; but Aunt Philippa, who had been dozing
in her easy-chair by the window, welcomed the
young man very kindly, and made him promise
to stay to dinner.

Mr. Tudor tried not to look too much
pleased as he accepted the invitation. A sort of
blush crossed his honest face as he turned to
me; he had two or three messages to deliver, he
said. Mr. Cunliffe had given him one, and Mrs.
Barton and Lady Betty. She, Lady Betty, wanted
me to know that Miss Darrell was going to
Brighton for a week or ten days, and that she
hoped that I should come home before then.

I heard too that Mr. Hamilton had gone
to Folkestone, and that he had tried to induce
Uncle Max to go with him. 'But it is no use

telling him he wants a change,' finished Mr. Tudor, with a sigh; 'he is bent on wearing himself out for other people.'

Mr. Tudor and I chatted on for the remainder of the afternoon. I had taken him out on the balcony—there were an awning and •some chairs, and we could sit there in the comparative privacy looking down on the passers-by. Aunt Philippa was nodding again—we could hear her regular breathing behind us; poor woman, she was worn out with bustle and gaiety. I was thankful that a grand horticultural *fête* kept all the aunts and cousins away, with the exception of the two who were riding with Jill.

Clayton brought us out some tea presently, and we found plenty of topics for conversation.

All at once I stopped in the middle of a conversation.

'Mr. Tudor, have my eyes deceived me, or was that Leah?'

'Who—what Leah? I do not know whom you mean!' he returned rather stupidly, staring in another direction. There was a cavalcade coming up the road—a tall slim girl, on a chestnut mare, riding on in front with a young man;

another girl and an elderly man with a grey moustache following them ; a groom bringing up the rear.

Of course it was Jill, smiling and waving towards the balcony ; she could not see Mr. Tudor under the awning, but she had caught sight of my silk dress. Jill looked very well . on horseback, people always turned round to watch her. She had a good seat and rode gracefully ; the dark habit suited her ; she braided her unmanageable locks into an invisible net that kept them tidy.

' Is that Miss Jocelyn ? ' asked Lawrence, almost in a voice of awe. The young curate grew very red as Jill rode under the balcony and nodded to him in a friendly manner.

' There is Mr. Tudor,' we heard her say. ' Be quick and lift me off my horse, Clarence.' But she had slipped to the ground before her cousin could touch her, and had run indoors.

Mr. Tudor went into the room at once, but I sat still for a moment. Why had I asked him ?—of course it was Leah. I could see her strange light-coloured eyes glancing up in my direction. What was she doing in London, I wondered. She was dressed well, evidently in her mistress's cast-off clothes, for she wore a handsome silk dress and mantle. Had they quarrelled and parted? I felt instinctively that it would be a good day for Gladwyn if Leah ever shook off its dust from her feet. Gladys regarded her as a spy and informer, and she had evidently an unwholesome influence over her mistress.

We separated soon after this to dress for dinner, and Mr. Tudor went to his hotel. I was rather sorry when I came downstairs to find that Jill had made rather a careless toilet. She wore the flimsy Indian muslin gown that I thought so unbecoming to her style, with a string of gold beads of curious Florentine work round her neck. She looked so different from the graceful young Amazon who had ridden up an hour ago that I felt provoked, and was not surprised to hear the old sharp tone in Aunt Philippa's voice—

'My dear Jocelyn, why have you put on that old gown? Surely your new cream-coloured dress with coffee lace would have been more suitable. What was Draper thinking about?'

'I was in too great a hurry; I did not wait for Draper,' returned Jill, candidly. 'Draper was dreadfully cross about it, but I ran away from her. What does it matter, mamma; they have all seen my cream-coloured dress, except—' But here Jill laughed; the naughty child meant Mr. Tudor.

'I am afraid there is not time to change it now; but I am very much vexed about it,' returned Aunt Philippa, in a loud whisper. 'You are really looking your worst to-night.' But Jill only laughed again, and asked her cousin Clarence when he took her down to dinner if it were not a very pretty gown.'

'I don't know much about gowns,' drawled the young man—Mr. Tudor and I were following them—'it looks rather flimsy and washed out. If I were you I would wear something more substantial. You see you are so big, Jocelyn; your habit suits you better.'

We heard Jill laughing in a shrill fashion at this dubious compliment, and presently she and Mr. Tudor, who sat next to her, were talking as happily as possible. I do not believe he noticed her unbecoming gown—his face had lighted up, and he was full of animation. Poor Lawrence, he was five-and-twenty, and yet the presence of this girl of sixteen was more to him than all the young ladyhood of Heathfield. Ever charming little Lady Betty was beaten out of the field by Jill's dark eyes and sprightly tongue.

It was a very pleasant evening, and we were all enjoying ourselves—no one imagined anything could or would happen ; life is just like that—we should just take up our candlesticks, we thought, and march off to bed when Aunt Philippa gave the signal. No one could have imagined that there would be a moment's deadly peril for one of the party—an additional thanksgiving for a life preserved that night.

And then no one seemed to know how it happened—people never do see somehow.

There was music going on. Agatha Chudleigh—the Chudleighs were Aunt Philippa's belongings—was playing the piano, and her brother Clarence was accompanying her on the violoncello. There was a little group round the piano. Jill was beating time, standing with her back to a small inlaid table, with a lamp on it. Mr. Tudor was beside her. Jill made a backward movement in her forgetfulness and enthusiasm. The next moment the music stopped with a crash. There was a cry of horror, the lamp seemed falling, glass smashed, liquid fire was pouring down Jill's unfortunate dress. If Mr. Tudor had not caught it, they said afterwards, with all that lace drapery, the room must have been in flames ; but he had jerked it back in its place, and snatching up a bear-skin rug that lay under the piano, had wrapped it round Jill. He was so strong and prompt, there was not a moment lost.

We had all crowded round in a moment, but no one dared to interfere with Mr. Tudor. We could hear Aunt Philippa sobbing with terror. Clarence Chudleigh extinguished the lamp, some one else flung an Indian blanket and a striped rug at Jill's feet. For one instant I could see the girl's face, white and rigid as a statue, as the young man's powerful arms enveloped her. Then the danger was over, and Jill was standing among us unhurt, with her muslin gown hanging in blackened shreds, and with bruises on her round white arms from the rough grip that had saved her life.

One instant's delay, and the fiery fluid must have covered her from head to foot ; if Lawrence had not caught the falling lamp, if he had lost one moment in smothering the lighted gown, she must have perished in agony before our eyes; but he was strong as a young Hercules, and, half suffocated and bruised as she was, Jill knew from what he had saved her.

As the scorched bear-skin dropped to the floor, Lawrence picked up the Indian blanket and flung it over Jill's tattered gown. 'Go up to your room, Miss Jocelyn,' he whispered; 'you are all right now,' and she obeyed without a word. Miss Gillespie and I followed. I think Aunt Philippa was faint or had palpitations, for I heard Uncle Brian calling loudly to some one to open the windows. Jill was hysterical as soon as she reached her room. She was quite unnerved and clung to me, shaking with sobs, while Miss Gillespie mixed some sal-volatile. I could not help crying a little with her from joy and thankfulness; but we got her quiet after a time, and took off the poor gown, and Jill showed us her bruises, and cheered up when we told her how brave and quiet she had been; and then she sat for some minutes with her face hidden in my lap, while I stroked her hair silently and thanked God in my heart for sparing our Jill.

Miss Gillespie had gone downstairs to carry a good report to Aunt Philippa. Directly she had gone, Jill jumped up still shaking a little, and went to her wardrobe.

'I must go downstairs,' she said a little feverishly, 'I have never thanked Mr. Tudor for saving my life. Help me to be quick, Ursie dear, for I feel so queer and tottery,' and nothing I could say would prevail on her to remain quietly in her room. While I was arguing with her, she had dragged out her ruby velveteen and was trying to fasten it with her trembling fingers.

'Oh, you are obstinate, Jill; you ought to be good on this night of all nights.' But she made no answer to this, and, seeing her bent on her own way, I brought her a brooch, and would have smoothed her hair, but she pushed me away.

'It does not matter how I look. I am only going down for a few minutes. He is going away, and I want to say good-night to him, and thank him,' and Jill walked downstairs rather unsteadily.

Mr. Tudor was just crossing the hall. When he saw Jill, he hurried up to her at once.

'Miss Jocelyn, this is very imprudent; you ought to have gone to bed, you are not fit to be up after such a shock,' looking at her pale face and swollen eyes with evident emotion.

Jill looked at him gently and seriously, and held out her hands to him quite simply.

'I could not go to bed without thanking you. I am not quite so selfish and thoughtless. You have saved my life—do you think I shall ever forget that?'

Poor Lawrence! the excitement, the terror, and relief were too much for him; and there was Jill holding his hands and looking up in his face, with her great eyes full of tears. It was not very wonderful that for a moment he forgot himself.

'I could not help doing it' he returned. 'What would have become of me if you had died? I could not have borne it.'

Jill drew her hands away, and her face looked a little paler in the moonlight. The young man's excited voice, his strange words, must have told her the truth. No, she was not too young to understand; her head drooped, and she turned away as she answered him.

'I shall always be grateful; good-night, Mr. Tudor—I must go to my mother; come, Ursula.' She did not look back as we walked across the hall, though poor Lawrence stood quite still watching us. Why had the foolish boy said that? Why had he forgotten his position and her youth? Why had he hinted that her life was necessary to his happiness? Would Jill ever forget those words, or the look that accompanied them? I felt almost angry with Lawrence as I followed Jill into the room.

Jill need never have doubted her mother's love. Aunt Philippa had been too faint and ill to follow her daughter to her room, but her face was quite beautiful with maternal tenderness as she folded the girl in her arms. Not even her father, who especially petted Jill, showed more affection for her that night.

'Oh, Jocelyn, my darling, are you quite sure that you are unhurt? Miss Gillespie says you were only frightened and a little bruised; but I wanted to see for myself. Mr. Tudor will not let us thank him, but we shall be grateful to him all our lives, my pet—what would your poor father and I have done without you?'

Jill hid her face like a baby on her mother's bosom—she was crying quietly—her interview with Mr. Tudor had certainly upset her. Uncle Brian put his hand in her rough locks. 'Never mind, my little girl, it is now over; you must go to bed and forget it,' which was certainly very good advice. I coaxed Aunt Philippa to let her go, and promised to remain with her until she was asleep. She was very quiet and hardly said a word as I helped her to undress, but as I sat down by the bedside, she drew my head down beside hers on the pillow.

'Don't think I am not grateful because I do not talk about it, Ursie dear,' she whispered. 'I hope to be better all my life for what has happened to-night.' But as Jill lay, with wide, solemn eyes, in the moonlight, I wondered what thoughts were coursing through her mind. Was she looking upon her life preserved as a life dedicated, regarding herself as set apart for higher work and nobler uses; or was her gratitude to her young preserver mixed with deeper and more mysterious feelings? I could not tell, but from that night I noticed a regular change in Jill—she became less girlish and fanciful, a new sort of womanliness developed itself, her high spirits were tempered with softness. Uncle Brian was right when he said a few days afterwards 'that his little girl was growing a woman.'

THE END OF THE SECOND VOLUME.

S.

Spottiswoode & Co. Printers, New-street Square, London.

www.ingramcontent.com/pod-product-compliance
Lightning Source LLC
Chambersburg PA
CBHW020943030726
47496CB00005B/1328